The sadness i... his heart.

He wanted to make Gina smile again. But she was talking about the husband she had lost, and it was obvious she was still hurting from that loss. That she still...loved that man?

Of course she does, he told himself. *They had been married for years. They had children together. She sees him in her baby boy. Little Barry even has his father's name. Her husband will always be a part of their lives, and that is only right.*

Still, it gave him an uncomfortable feeling. Almost as if...there was no room for him in the equation? But he was just a colleague, as he had said himself. He could become a friend, maybe. That was all.

He wanted to take the pain away if he could. But he couldn't. Gina should meet a man like her husband had been, who could give her that romantic fantasy all over. What use was a loner to her, an outdoor man who lacked social graces, who lived in a simple cabin, who worked in the very mountains that represented the essence of her grief? That were covered with the snow that had stolen her happiness away from her with the avalanche that had killed Barry.

Ewan was of the mountains, and Gina was of the valley. That was right...wasn't it?

Dear Reader,

Thank you so much for picking up the latest book in my Heroes of the Rockies series! If you read the first two, *Winning Over the Rancher* and *The Rancher Resolution*, you have already met Gina Williams, her adorable twin daughters, Stacey and Ann, and baby Barry. Gina went through a lot, and she really deserves a happy ending with a wonderful man who understands her but also challenges her to look beyond the worry and self-doubt that have plagued her since the heartache of her husband's death.

I'm a fan of hiking, wildlife and mountains, and it was especially fun for me to take Gina and her children away from the ranch to the great outdoors, where they find friendship, confidence and, above all, love. I hope you also enjoy the escape from your everyday life for a few hours to admire the greatness of nature and realize once more that no matter what happens in your life, there is always a new tomorrow filled with hope.

Warmest wishes,

Viv

A DAD FOR THE TWINS

VIV ROYCE

Harlequin

HEARTWARMING

H Harlequin®
HEARTWARMING™

Recycling programs
for this product may
not exist in your area.

ISBN-13: 978-1-335-05144-8

A Dad for the Twins

H Harlequin Enterprises ULC
22 Adelaide St. West, 41st Floor
Toronto, Ontario M5H 4E3, Canada
www.Harlequin.com

Printed in Lithuania

MIX
Paper | Supporting
responsible forestry
FSC® C021394

Viv Royce writes uplifting feel-good stories set in tight-knit communities where people fend for each other and love saves the day. If she can fit in lots of delicious food and cute pets, all the better. When she's not plotting the next scene, she can be found crafting, playing board games and trying new ice cream.

Books by Viv Royce

Harlequin Heartwarming

Heroes of the Rockies

Winning Over the Rancher
The Rancher Resolution

ACKNOWLEDGMENTS

As always, thanks to all authors (especially Harlequin authors), editors and agents who share online about the writing and publishing process. Special mention goes to my amazing agent, Jill Marsal, my wonderful editor, Adrienne Macintosh, whose feedback is always spot-on, and to the rest of the dedicated team at Harlequin Heartwarming, especially the cover-design team for the evocative cover.

The tourist-information center in this story is fictional but inspired by real-life centers in the Rockies. The people that work there make these centers such a joy to visit and learn about nature. If you are ever near such a center, do drop by and have a look around—it's worth it!

CHAPTER ONE

WITH SLOW PRECISE MOVEMENTS, Gina Williams Roberts swept the broom across the wooden boards outside the open shop doors. The Western store was one of the largest businesses on Main Street, and like most others it was built in authentic country style with lots of wood and painted details. Sweeping was her first task in the morning, and it formed a sort of calming routine to the start of the day. Soon the store would be buzzing with customers looking for hats, belts and buckles, or going through the vintage music collection in the back corner. Locals bought saddle wax from their favorite brands, while visitors loved to dress up their kids with junior-sized cowboy hats and boots. Even babies found Western-themed outfits here.

From inside, a cheerful male voice resounded, "It is a beautiful spring morning here in Heartmont, Colorado. And whether you're tuning in as a resident or a tourist looking to enjoy our amazing Rocky Mountains and the area's small towns full of heart, welcoooooome—" he stretched the o with the boom of a ship's horn "—to Boulder County and to the beats of this country classic..."

As fiddles began playing a riveting tune, Gina tapped along. It wouldn't be her personal choice to have music on this early, and to be honest, she'd rather sweep in silence breathing the stillness of the morning deep into her being.

But as her boss, Bud Travers, liked to have the local station playing, at full volume when the store was open, she had to turn on the radio each morning and accept the music and the local news as part of her everyday routine. She was just an employee here and couldn't make any decisions. Not about the music or the window displays. It was a shame because she had so many ideas. But this was someone else's business, not hers. She had grown to accept that and told herself with a smile that this vigorous sweeping left and right counted as a free workout. What job offered such privileges?

There, almost done. She moved to the edge of the wooden boards and stood a moment to look left and right down the street. Around this time of day most businesses were opening up, and her fellow shopkeepers were pulling out chalkboards with offers written in large lettering and twined baskets with goods on sale, lining them up along their property. From the open doors of the bakery across the street the inviting scent of freshly baked bread and sweet treats filled the air.

Mrs. Jenkins, who owned the general store, was about to go into the bakery—probably to get the cinnamon buns she and her husband always ate with their eleven o'clock coffee. She raised a hand in greeting and Gina waved back.

Having grown up here, she had known Mrs. Jenkins and the other townsfolk all her life. Heartmont had been that small-town community where you could easily stick around. Her parents had probably bet she would marry some local guy and tend a farm just like theirs. Apple orchards, a few cattle. Or maybe something with a corn maze and educational activities, as young farmers did these days to attract passing tourists. Her parents had never imagined that she'd marry a city slicker and move away. She hadn't thought she would, either, until she had met Barry.

Her hands tensed on the broom handle for a moment. Thinking about him had become easier over time. In the beginning, right after he had died, it had been so hard to even hear his name or recall his voice, or if the phone rang, to remember it couldn't be him as he would never call her again. She would never hear him say "I love you" or "Kiss the girls for me."

He had died far away from home, in the mountains where he'd been skiing with friends. An avalanche had caught him and swept him away, burying all Gina's hopes and dreams right along with him. A few moments in time had changed everything, making her a widow, and a pregnant widow at that. Instead of welcoming her husband back into her arms for hugs and kisses, and the sweet planning for the arrival of their newborn, she had prepared for his burial, while trying to explain to her distraught daughters that Daddy wasn't coming home again. The twins had been real Daddy's girls, and it had been hard on both of them to deal with the grief. Stacey, the wilder one, had become even more daring and hard to control, while Ann, who had always been quieter and more thoughtful, had had a head full of questions and fears about dying. Looking at their sad little faces had been almost harder than dealing with her own pain.

Gina took a deep breath, trying to loosen

the inevitable tightening in her chest as she remembered how her little family had been torn apart. Yes, they had suffered hard knocks, and grief had a way of sneaking back up on you when you least expected it, but she had to focus on the good things. On the progress they had made. Together.

They had a good life here, on the ranch where Gina had grown up, the ranch now tended by her brother Cade, with the help of Mom and Cade's new wife, Lily. It was wonderful that Cade, who had always been a loner, had fallen in love with Gina's best friend—also Barry's sister—when Lily had visited the ranch to see how Gina and the girls were doing after the loss. Sometimes Gina still couldn't believe how that first visit, and Lily's subsequent offer of help to rebuild the ranch after storm damage, had changed all of their lives so profoundly. Cade had found the love of his life, someone to stand by him in good and bad times, to share his passion for the orchards and all the animals that lived on the ranch. For Lily, it had been a big change to leave the city and her career in marketing behind and settle in the countryside. But she had made friends quickly, since she was always cheerful, thinking of solutions instead of problems. After her marriage to Cade last summer, she had really found her own place in the community and on the ranch. She was there for Gina whenever she wanted to talk and was wonderful with the girls. It was good to have family to rely on and not have to raise the kids all by herself.

But, Gina had to admit to herself in the quiet moments when she contemplated her life, being around family was also a constant reminder of everything she had lost. Seeing her brother so happy in his marriage, being able to do things with his wife instead of alone, made her feel the emptiness in her own life all the more. She tried to fight that feeling, thinking it was unfair to Cade, who had helped her out when Barry had died and she had lost her home and belongings because of debts that had suddenly come to light. Unbeknownst to Gina, Barry had accumulated a mountain of debt to pay for their high-end lifestyle, and once he had passed away, the list of what she owed had grown ever longer. She had been forced to sell the pizzeria that she and Barry had taken over from his parents, making her feel like a total business failure. Then she had also been forced to sell her house and most of her belongings, stripping away any security she had left. The girls had been terrified, and she hadn't known how she could be a good mother to them when she couldn't even provide a roof over their heads. It had knocked her self-confidence down to next to nothing, until Cade had stepped in.

He had selflessly taken her into his house, cared for her and the girls, helped them back onto their feet. He had provided the safe haven she needed to recover from all the shocks, have her baby boy and focus on her little family without the pressure of having to bring in money. Now that she was gradually regaining her independence, she felt even more grateful that he had given her this chance to rebuild her life. She wanted him to have all the happiness in the world because he really deserved it. She owed him and Mom so much. She was so grateful to them and counted herself lucky to have such caring family members.

But sometimes it was just incredibly hard to sit at the table and watch Cade and Lily tease each other and laugh and slap each other with tea towels as they did the dishes, and know she had had all that with Barry but it was over. To know that she would never feel that way again.

That seemed obvious. She had loved him so much, had fallen head over heels for him. She could never ever feel that way again. She was older now, wiser. Toughened up by life. More…fearful perhaps?

No, she'd rather call it cautious. Which was only smart when you were a widowed mother of three and had responsibility for your children's future. Coming back to Heartmont with nothing had been hard. Rebuilding some kind of life even harder. She had cried at night when she was all alone in her room, not knowing how she would ever manage. But she had done it. She had found a job here in Bud's store, earned her own money to contribute to their communal life on the ranch. Maybe one day it would be enough to get her own place in town. She dreamed about that sometimes. Having her own household again.

It was nice on the ranch. It was handy to have someone around all the time to watch the girls and little Barry, the cute baby boy they all adored. It was convenient and easy and… yet she wanted more. A little independence. Freedom to make her own decisions…and her own mistakes?

Gina swallowed hard. She turned away from the street abruptly to carry the broom inside. Her secret dreams of her own business were nice and all, but they had to stay that: dreams. She couldn't risk investing money in some undertaking that could go wrong. Her little family had already lost everything once. She had been hunted by debtors. She'd never go through that again.

Or put her children through that insecurity.

A car horn honked, and she turned to see who it was. Her boss's old Mercedes came to a screeching halt in front of the steps leading to the store, and he jumped out and waved at her. His characteristic cowboy hat, an example of what he sold in the store, sat askew on his head and he looked very excited. Maybe he had closed a big deal and they'd be busy all day getting everything packed up for the order? She hoped it was something like that to take her thoughts off her unrest. Her life was good now and she shouldn't rock the boat with silly wishes.

"I need to talk to you," Bud said as he passed her with long strides. "Is the coffee ready?"

One of her first activities when she came in was to make coffee. Bud said she made a mean pot, which was the biggest compliment in his book.

"Yes, it should be ready by now," she assured him.

He was in the kitchen area already and she heard mugs clang. She put the broom away and checked her appearance in the small mirror on the inside of the broom closet door. Her face was flushed with the exertion and the fresh wind outside, but her eyes looked a little worried. She forced a smile onto her face. Bud liked a warm welcome for his customers.

She came back into the store's main room and found her boss at the counter with his trademark mug with bulls' horns. Sipping his coffee with an appreciative grunt, he gestured with his free hand to another mug sitting ready for her. Although she didn't really want any coffee right now, she came over and picked up the steaming mug. Blowing into it, she said, "It's a beautiful morning, isn't it?"

"It is, it is." Bud nodded weightily as he transferred the mug from one hand to the other. "I dropped off the order at Stephenson's and he showed me a newborn calf. Pretty little thing. He joked he would call it Bud, but I hope for the little one it will be something better." He shifted his weight and stared past her.

Gina gave him a suspicious look. Her boss was a direct man who never beat around the bush. But it definitely looked like he was stalling now.

Her heart skipped a beat. Would there be some bad news? Something he was reluctant to tell her? Had a customer complained about her? Or had she made a mistake packing orders?

See, she told herself, *this is what I mean. You jump at the slightest indication of trouble. Even if you made a mistake, Bud is the one who has to deal with the complaint or even the damage. You don't have to do that yourself; you are not responsible. That would be different if you had your own business. You couldn't handle the stress. So be glad you work here.*

"Look, Gina," Bud said, "I don't really know how to tell you this any other way than by just saying it. I can't keep you here."

She stared at him. Within a split second after thinking she was happy she had a job, she lost it? Just like that?

But why?

Bud said, "I thought about this long and hard, and it's just a too big a chance to let it pass me by. I have to do it. And to do it I have to close the store."

"Close the store?" Gina echoed. She blinked rapidly trying to understand what he meant. But her head was flooding with panic and she had trouble focusing. "You sound just like the twins when they are all excited and want to tell me something. They start in the middle of the tale and I don't understand any of it. Why would you have to close the store? Business is good, right?"

"Oh, business is fine. But you see, without me here to take care of everything… I can't leave you to deal with the… You don't have the experience, and besides, it takes too much time. You have three children."

"I still don't understand," Gina said. Her knees were wobbly, and she took a big sip of coffee, hoping it would calm her a little. The doorbell jangled indicating the arrival of a customer, but she didn't look to see who it was. She just wanted to know more.

Bud seemed equally focused on the conversation. He put his mug down, planted his feet apart as if he geared up for something and said, "Well, it's like this. A friend of mine left the county years ago and started a Western experience in Texas. It's like a little Western town where you can stay and see all kinds of shows at the saloon and the sheriff's office and more. He has been asking me ever since to come and spend some time with him, be a part of it, as he knows I'm even more of a Western fan than he is. Now, I've been putting it off, thinking I can't just close up the store for a few months and go, but lately I've been asking myself, why not? What am I waiting for? I'm not getting any younger. If I want to make something of my life, see a little more of the world, I have to do it now. So I asked my suppliers to put deliveries on hold for a while, and I arranged to make any necessary payments while I am away. And… I guess I thought that maybe I couldn't get it organized and it would be a convenient excuse not to do it, but everyone was very cooperative and encouraging so… It's all done. I wrote my buddy an email this morning that I'm coming, and here I am now, to tell you, my valued employee, that I'm closing up the store and…" He made a hand gesture. "I do realize it's a big change for you to suddenly be out of work, but… You're welcome to start again once I'm back. I just don't know when I will be back, yet."

Gina stared at her boss in disbelief. Bud Travers was a man of habits, who led his life like a well-oiled machine. He liked things a certain way, the radio on, his coffee strong, bingo on Friday nights. He never took a vacation; he lived for his work and his small-town enjoyments. And now he suddenly wanted to leave for Texas and… This couldn't be happening.

She said softly, "Are you sure you really

want to do this? I can understand your friend
has been asking you to drop by sometime, and
you can go over for a few days, a brief break
from work here... I can take care of the store
for a week or so and..."

"No, Gina." Bud put his hand on her arm
in a friendly gesture to stop her speaking. "I
have to go away for a longer time. Have to do
something for me. I've been...stuck in a rut
here. I love this town and the people. Believe
me, I didn't make this decision lightly. It became clear to me over time that the wind of
change needs to blow through my life. If I let
you run the store and I manage it from a distance, I will still be doing the same old things I
always did. I have to do it differently. I'm sorry
that it also touches you, and I guess I should
have involved you in my plans sooner, but I
didn't want you to worry about it before I was
certain I could get everything in order. I just
cleared the last hurdle and I raced over here
to tell you. Also, you live with your brother
so you don't need the money to pay rent or a
mortgage and..."

Gina forced a smile even though this last
remark felt like an added blow. That was the
way people in town looked at her? She lived

with her brother, nice and easy—no rent, no mortgage, no responsibility...

She bit her lip. She didn't want to feel this way. Bud meant well, Cade meant well, everyone had the best for her in mind. But sometimes she just wished that she could live her own life, feel like she was in control. After Barry's death, she had spun away from the person she had been. The person who had been redecorating the pizzeria and thinking up ways to promote it. The person who had started a communal garden and had brought people from her neighborhood together to grow their own vegetables and flowers and take care of abandoned animals. Back then she had felt confident and capable, but after Barry's death somehow she had become smaller. More careful, more fearful, keeping more to herself. Never chasing a new idea and experiencing the pure joy of making it work. And she didn't want to live that way. Not deep down inside.

Bud said, "I guess people will be surprised when I put up the sign."

"What sign?" Gina asked.

"Oh, it's in the car. I made it right before I drove out here. To make it real. I'll get it." He ran off, almost giddy, like a teenager going on a first date. She couldn't believe this was her boss. It seemed like another person.

He came back quickly, holding up a cardboard sign. He turned it over to her and she read, "Closed for an indefinite time, owner on adventure."

She blinked hard to see if the word was really there. *Adventure?* It sounded like something kids indulged in, not responsible adults.

Bud said, "I'll put this up Friday afternoon. I'm flying to Texas on Saturday."

Gina felt the floor move under her feet. "That soon?" He had mentioned that he'd been planning this for a while, but still she had thought he would go in the summer or… That she would have some time to adjust to the whole idea. Some time to find another job. But now it seemed that by the end of this week she'd be jobless.

The idea made panic rise in her chest. No job meant no money and no money meant no way to pay bills. Bud might say she lived with her brother anyway, but she did contribute to life on the ranch and save to buy the girls nice clothes and afford days out. How could he take that security away from her?

"I need to meet with a few people before I leave," Bud said. "To hand them all the information they need to take over from me on the committees and stuff."

Bud liked to have a finger in every pie when it came to decisions about their town, and he sat on the council, and in committees dealing with festivities and development, so his departure would create shock waves around town, she supposed. People might have known he toyed with the idea of leaving for a time, but to actually do it... This news would get tongues wagging in upcoming days.

He didn't wait for a response but shouted a goodbye and hurried off. Once he had vanished and there was nothing around her but the country music from the radio, she almost felt like this whole episode hadn't happened. It couldn't have. It was out of character for him, it was...

Too hard to believe.

But he had left his sign on the counter, and it really said that the store was closing. Because of adventure.

Adventure. The word seemed to mock her. Sure, Bud was going on an adventure, and she was left to deal with the consequences. She didn't know whether she wanted to stamp her foot in anger or hide her face in her hands and cry. This was so...unexpected. So strange.

"Are you alright?" a friendly male voice asked.

She spun round to face a tall man with broad shoulders and a full head of dark hair. His kind brown eyes looked her over with concern. He wore an all-green outfit she associated with outdoorsy people. Perhaps a tourist?

Her gaze dropped to his feet to see if he wore hiking boots. He did, and beside him, half hiding behind his legs, was the fluffiest, cutest small dog she had ever seen. An involuntary *aw* escaped her and she dropped to her knees to reach out for the dog's little head. That chocolate brown fur had to be so soft.

"Careful," he warned, "she's very shy."

Gina stopped her gesture midair and just smiled at the dog. "Hello, little one. You are so pretty. Yes, you are totally gorgeous. How are you? What's your name?"

"We don't know her name, but we gave her a new one. Fuzzy, because of her curls. Someone left her at the tourist center. Judging by her size and all that fluff, you'd think she's a puppy, but she's actually quite an elderly dog. Which is probably why the owner wanted to get rid of her. Just tied her to a tree and left."

"How heartless." Gina looked up at him. "Who would do such a thing?"

"There can be reasons. Elderly dogs need special food and there can be vet bills to pay. Sometimes money is tight, and people do things that they normally wouldn't do."

Gina felt a flush rise in her cheeks. When she had been in debt, she had sometimes pushed past other people in the supermarket to get to discounted products. She had told lies to cover the fact that she didn't have the money for certain expenses. It had been so painful and difficult. It had eaten away at her self-esteem. Was it so hard to understand that sometimes people became desperate and did things that they might later regret?

"She's found a good place to stay now," he said with warmth in his voice. "The past doesn't matter anymore."

"The past always matters. It makes us who we are." Gina rose to her feet, avoiding looking him in the eye. "You call the dog shy, but she could just be afraid because her owner left her and broke her trust. How are you going to get her to have faith in you?"

"By showing her that I am trustworthy. Not one day, not one week, but always."

"Always?" She almost scoffed. "That's a big promise."

"But one I intend to keep."

She suppressed the urge to laugh. Barry had made so many promises—to her, to the girls—all with warmth in his voice, love in his eyes. He had meant it, but he hadn't been able to keep his word. In his urge to provide for them and give them everything, he had spent too much money and thrown them into an abyss of debt. He had meant well, but he had made such a mess of it.

That was how people were. How life was, maybe. But you could guard yourself against it. Watch your back, protect your kids.

"How can I help you?" she asked in a professional voice.

"Actually, I came in to ask Bud to give a lecture at the tourist information center where I work. But…" A suntanned hand landed on the sign on the counter, his finger running over the word *adventure*. "I see he's not available?"

If he had come in when the bell jangled, he had probably overheard part of the conversation. There was no point in denying it. Bud was right now spreading the news around town. Like any exciting tidbit it would get around fast. "I'm afraid he's leaving for a while." Even putting it into words made her heart sink again.

The man nodded solemnly. "I see. Well, I

still have some business here, because I also wanted to ask you something."

"Me?" Gina looked at him now, intrigued. "But we don't know each other, do we?"

"No, we don't." He reached out his hand. "Ewan McAllister. Like I said, I work at the tourist information center in Hillock. Maybe you know it?"

Gina nodded. "I've been there a few times, as a girl. Not recently."

The tourist information center sat at the foot of the Rockies, and since Barry had died in an avalanche, she wasn't too keen on mountains and snow. She avoided things that reminded her of his accident and the ruin it had caused in her life.

"Well, you might remember we have a little shop there and we sell all kinds of products the tourists might be interested in. Notebooks, bookmarks, pencils with animal toppers, but also honey, tea and cookies. Now, I heard you make delicious apple muffins, buns and pies. So I thought you could deliver them to us and we can sell them there."

Gina's mouth almost fell open. It was true that she made apple products, partly because there were so many apples at the ranch and partly because she loved cooking and baking.

It provided a nice diversion from her day job and the often hectic times with the children. It brought her calm and joy. She had sometimes thought it would be wonderful to do more of it. To do it professionally.

Actually, she had sometimes thought she'd have exchanged her job at Bud's store for a little business of her own anytime if she hadn't worried so much about money. About finding takers for her products.

And now this man made her this offer?

He was still holding out his hand and she hurried to put hers in it. "Gina Williams. But you probably knew that already?"

Around town she always used her maiden name. People knew her that way and automatically called her that, since she'd grown up here.

He nodded. "I know you've been living on the Williams ranch for a while. With your children. You have two little girls, right, and a baby boy?"

"Barry is eighteen months already. He's hardly a baby anymore," she said with a wistful smile. "They grow up so fast."

It felt good to have his warm, solid grasp around her hand and to see the genuine interest in his brown eyes. But why would a perfect stranger be interested in her family life? Men usually didn't gush over babies. Especially not babies they didn't even know.

Why would he ask her to sell products at the tourist information center? There had to be some catch, but she had no idea what it could be.

She gently pulled her hand free and straightened up a little. "I uh… I do make products on occasion and have sold them at farmers markets and events, but I've never made them in large quantities and—"

"But with Bud leaving town and the store closing, you will have more time for it," he interjected kindly. "I'm sure Granny Grant would love to have your apple products as addition to the store."

"Granny Grant?" she queried, not remembering ever having heard the name.

"She owns the building that houses the tourist center. In fact, she owns a large section of land there. The Grants were among the first families to settle in the region."

"Oh, I think I remember my dad telling me about that when we visited the center when I was little." Gina tried to remember what exactly he had said. "There were a few families who settled here and built Heartmont and the surrounding towns. Didn't most of them come from Scotland?"

"That's right. My name is testimony to that legacy." He smiled. "McAllister is Scottish alright. So is Ewan. When you go right back to the origins of the name, it means 'of the mountain.' And I love mountains."

Gina forced herself to keep smiling. That was just great. She met a man who offered her a job, just when she needed one, and he loved mountains and she hated them. What a great combination.

But then, she didn't have to go into the mountains. She only had to create apple products and have them delivered to the tourist information center. She could even ask someone else to deliver them so she didn't have to go there herself.

That was doable, she supposed.

"You should come over some time and have a look at the center, meet Granny and some other people." he suggested. "Then you can see for yourself what kind of shop it is and what we already sell and how your products might fit in. And as you have experience working in a shop—" he gestured around him "—you could also help selling things, for starters, on busier days like weekends or during spring break. And once summer comes, we will have even more tourists on our hands so there will be more work. Why don't you come this Saturday? Then you can bring the children. I'm sure they would love to see the animals we have and learn a little about the Rockies."

"Animals?" Gina echoed. Her head was spinning. She didn't want to go anywhere near the Rockies, and now he was inviting her over for a visit, next Saturday, with the kids.

Everything inside her rebelled against the idea. Her children weren't going anywhere near mountains. No way. Stacey would get all wild and want to do adventurous stuff. Ann might start asking questions again about Daddy and how he had died. And little Barry... He was too young to understand much of it, but she just didn't want to expose him to the tension that would accompany such a visit.

"Mounted animals," he said. "We show examples of animals that live in the Rockies, like white-tailed deer, elk and mountain lions. Kids love to see them, touch the fur."

"Oh, yes, I remember the mounted animals." Dad had taken her along the displays and explained how each animal lived. "I always found them a little intimidating."

"I'll make sure I'm there to show you around

and make it fun for the kids. They won't be afraid."

He really made easy promises. Maybe kids who came from other backgrounds found it fun. But he didn't know about their family situation, their past. She had created safety for them now, and she didn't want that disrupted.

She swallowed hard. "I don't know."

"Think about it. And if you feel like it, give me a call." He reached out and took a Post-it note that lay on the counter to scribble his phone number on it. As he was at it, Fuzzy reached out a hesitant snout to sniff Gina's leg. She raised her head and looked up at her. Then she made a soft, almost pleading sound. It was as if the dog was...asking her to come?

That was really far-fetched. The dog had no idea about what they had just discussed.

"Fuzzy seems to like you," Ewan said as he put his pen back into his pocket. "It would be helpful to have her around people she likes." He held out the Post-it to Gina. "Think about it, okay?"

She took a deep breath and then accepted the note. His fingers brushed hers a moment, and again she had that odd sensation as if he provided some kind of...solidness. A sense she could depend on him. But she didn't even know him.

He reached down to scratch Fuzzy behind her ears. "Come on, girl, we have to do some grocery shopping for Granny."

Fuzzy seemed reluctant to leave. She looked up at Gina again. Gina sat on her haunches and let her hand dangle before her, close to the floor. The dog reached out and carefully sniffed it. Then she made another soft, almost coaxing sound.

"What did I say? She likes you." Ewan looked down at them with a broad smile. "She would love to see you Saturday." He gave the leash a little tug, and Fuzzy followed him to the door. About to go out, he turned and said, still smiling, "We both would."

As the twosome vanished from sight, Gina had the same sensation she'd had when Bud left. That none of this could be true. It had happened so suddenly, and it took her by surprise. She didn't like to feel uncertain.

And this man really befuddled her. He had such an easy way with people, and the way he had taken in the stray dog was just… The warmth seeping through her was something she hadn't felt in a long time.

A long, long time.

She stared at the sign on the counter. At the word *adventure*. Maybe people did need a change once in a while. A step outside the set boundaries.

A…breath of fresh air?

Could it hurt so much to just go and see his tourist information center? Take the kids and have an afternoon off? She remembered she had really loved it when she was little. Some time away from the ranch, just her and her dad. It had felt special.

The animals hadn't been intimidating really, just awe-inspiring. And there had been a little café with lemonade and coloring books. Everything children liked. The girls could use a trip. An inexpensive one that would still be fun.

She'd take a look around, meet a few people and… Then she could decide later what to do about his offer to come sell her apple products in their shop.

She relaxed her tight hands and exhaled in a huff.

Take it slowly. You can do that.

Just one step at a time.

CHAPTER TWO

WHEN EWAN PARKED his car outside the information center, his mind was busy with a little plan to get Gina's products into Granny's store. Gina might also be able to lend a hand organizing a few things on the days she delivered her baked goods. Granny, the kind elderly lady, could use a pair of extra hands, even if she would never admit it. She liked her independence and would be angry if she thought he was forcing help onto her. He had to tread very carefully here.

Besides, Granny's store was already chockfull with all kinds of products and this wasn't the top season for sales. Actually spring was more of a quiet time, a transition from winter when people descended on the area to ski and snowboard, and summer when the Rockies attracted families for outdoor activities like camping, hiking and rafting. Right now there was still some snow, but it wasn't the best,

while the temperatures weren't high enough
for more summery events.

It was the in-between season Ewan loved
because it gave him a chance to breathe and to
enjoy the environment where he worked without the constant pressure of yet another tour to
guide. He did enjoy being busy, and he would
certainly not want his days to be empty and
stretch ahead without anything to do, but it
was also good to plan some stuff on his own
and not...be with people all day long.

Ewan smiled to himself. Fact was, he wasn't
a people person. Not deep down. Anyone who
had seen him at work, giving tours and chatting with everyone from the elderly to the
smallest children, might guess otherwise, but
Ewan was a bit of a loner. It was almost inevitable after being raised by two world travelers
who thought the best places were the most remote on the planet. He had lived for months
without seeing people besides his parents, and
it had felt perfectly fine. He had been secure in
the lap of their little family, had learned new
things, had enjoyed breathtaking views, and he
had never actually missed social interaction.

His grandparents back in the US had worried about the little boy growing up without
friends his own age, but he had never felt

shortchanged by his childhood. On the contrary, he had been privileged to visit countries other American children only heard about in school. He had seen wild animals, experienced the forces of nature up close. It had been wonderful, and he wouldn't change a thing about it. But after he had left his parents to their next travel adventure and had gone out to forge his own path in life, he had sensed that maybe there had been a downside to the life he had led so far.

It was easy for him to say hi and chat with someone, share a few superficial facts about the natural surroundings or the plans he had made, but it was hard to have any kind of deep and meaningful conversation. To begin with, he simply didn't have any close long-term friends. No childhood buddies that he had played with in the sandbox, no guys he had met in college. He had never spent summer nights at the beach with people his own age philosophizing about life. He had gotten a degree in wildlife management, sure, but that education had been done all over the world, partly online, partly attending classes in person in Asia, Africa and South America. His classmates had changed every few months, and he had never been able to build friendships that lasted beyond the next move. It had broadened his horizon and given him unique knowledge, but it had been hard, maybe even impossible, to form a bond with people he was only close to for a few weeks or months. He could look classmates up on social media, of course, to see what they were up to now, and he had even donated some money for a bird sanctuary two of them had set up, but that was all so superficial. His parents were trekking through Asia with limited access to the internet. And he was used to only receiving the odd email and writing a few words in reply that would probably not reach them for weeks anyway. They did what they loved, and he did the same, so what was wrong with that?

But still, at the start of the new year he had sat down and realized that at thirty-four, he really didn't have any close relationships, and he mostly didn't even mind.

Maybe it just wasn't in his nature to confide in others. He liked to watch from the sidelines, observe, deduce, conclude. He didn't easily ask for an opinion or partake in a communal project. He was perfectly happy working on his own.

And to stay balanced, he needed time alone. So working here at the information center was

just perfect. He could lend a hand with any
chore that came up—after all, if you had lived
as primitively as he had, it wasn't a big deal
to climb on a roof and fix a few boards or get
a jack and change a flat tire. And any time he
felt a bit shut in by all the coziness of too many
people, he could go out and be alone among the
majestic snowcapped mountains. Watch birds,
look for animal tracks on the dirt paths. Feel
like he was the only human being in a grand
canopy of trees and stars.

But now suddenly his peace and quiet was
invaded by a woman with the most beautiful
eyes he had ever seen. Eyes that seemed to
have looked up to him for help. For a solution
to her problem. And he had offered one without
hesitating. Her products could work perfectly
at the center because they were made from
produce from the region, created at a multi-
generational family ranch. People enjoyed such
a personal touch when they took home a little
gift or reminder of their stay. He had meant
what he had said to her, and he wasn't sorry
that he had invited her to come over on Saturday. It was just that he realized now, looking
at the half-full parking lot, that there weren't a
ton of tourists to buy what was already in the
shop, and Granny might not be overenthusias-

tic about adding more to the offer. Especially
food items that had limited shelf life. A scarf
could hang on the rack for years, but freshly
baked muffins and apple pies...

*Man, McAllister, what did you get yourself
into?*

Ewan shook his head as he let Fuzzy out
of the car. She jumped onto the ground and
shook herself, then looked up at him with a
wise gaze. Her expression echoed his own sen-
timents. As if she also wanted to say: How are
you going to solve this?

He leaned down to scratch her behind the
ears. "Now, what choice did I have, huh?
Wouldn't you have offered help to such a nice
lady? Come on, you want to see her again.
Admit it. And I had to think of something to
lure her here. She didn't look overeager to say
yes..."

"Good morning!" The cheerful voice boomed
into his ear. Turning his head, Ewan's gaze first
struck huge muddy boots, then traveled up tall
legs and a broad chest to finally find the round
face with a gray, wild tousled beard and wide
smile. Garrett Lewis's nickname at the center
was Grizzly, both for the messy beard and his
bear-like posture. He worked as a handyman,
wood artist and mountain guide. He wasn't a

man of many words, but Ewan had gotten to know him as utterly reliable and with a heart of gold. Still, the man couldn't resist cracking jokes at Ewan's fondness for Fuzzy, whose appearance suggested she should be curled up in a basket by the fire rather than on the road with a sturdy mountain ranger.

"When I see you talking to that dog," Grizzly said sweetly, "I could swear you think she understands your every word."

"She does," Ewan said with as much dignity as he could muster. He could only hope Grizzly hadn't overheard him mentioning a nice lady, or there would be no end to his teasing. "Dogs are very sensitive."

Grizzly nodded slowly. "I must say she's doing well after being abandoned. I thought such a little scrap of a dog would be traumatized."

"She found a loving home here. I guess you could say she was abandoned to the right place." Ewan clicked the leash onto Fuzzy's collar and straightened up. It struck him now that Gina Williams had also been abandoned by her boss, left out in the cold by his sudden impetuous decision to leave for Texas, close up his business that was her only livelihood. But like little Fuzzy by his side, she might have been abandoned to find her way to the right place in life. This center where so many people who had all suffered their share of heartache had found meaningful work, companionship. Soon they would celebrate its anniversary: seventy-five years of teaching people about the wonders of nature. A lot of hands were needed to prepare for all the festivities, and Ewan had been determined from the start to make this the best season ever for the center. They depended on the income the tourists brought in to keep the center going. Especially for Granny, who had devoted her life to educating people about wildlife and the importance of preserving this beautiful natural world. As costs rose, it became more difficult to balance the expenses with the income from sales and tours, and he sometimes saw a pensive look in her eyes he didn't like. She had to be happy here, unburdened by worries about keeping the center alive. They all had to chip in, do their part to make sure the center could last another seventy-five years, at least.

Now having met Gina, he saw a chance to involve her in that project. Her products would be a fresh new addition to their offerings, and he bet she could also deliver some great input on the anniversary program. Maybe it was all…meant to be?

Grizzly clapped a large hand on his shoulder. "You're just in time for a cup of Granny's mocha, friend. I think I can already smell it." He inhaled so hard his nostrils flared.

Ewan laughed. "If Granny has been busy, there won't be any coffee unless you make it yourself."

Grizzly sighed exaggeratedly. "A man can dream." He squeezed Ewan's shoulder. "A man can dream." It seemed his words carried a deeper meaning than just being about the desired coffee. But surely Grizzly couldn't know what Ewan had been thinking. What he had been up to in town…

It was a shame, though, that Grizzly had popped up and would be drinking coffee with Granny and Ewan as Ewan had meant to feel out whether she was open to adding Gina's products. But with Grizzly present he didn't know exactly how to broach the subject without immediately attracting unwanted attention.

They walked down the path to the main entrance's glass doors. The building had stood here since the late '40s of the previous century, built from stone and timber, and had served the public in one way or another for almost seventy-five years. It had started modestly and grown over the years, adding every more services to its offer. Currently, it flew the state flag and the special Rocky Mountain Wilderness Information Point flag used by all information centers spread across the region. Each center offered the public a chance to learn something about nature, but most were smaller, with just basic facilities and a ranger, like himself, present on weekends and holidays only. This center had a large room downstairs with mounted animals and information plaques, a quiz to take on a computer, a counter with coffee and snacks and access to rangers 24/7 for emergencies like forest fires or rescues. Helicopters could swiftly take first responders to remote spots from a nearby pad.

Ewan was on the list of those regularly on call to assist. When tourists went missing, he was flown out by helicopter to their last known location and tracked them on foot from there. He knew the area intimately and had basic first aid skills to keep people comfortable until they could be moved.

Grizzly swept open both glass doors and called, "Granny! Where is the morning energy boost?"

To their left was a wooden counter with

racks of information flyers on top. A middle-aged woman stood behind it, staring down at the cell phone in her hand. Grizzly waved at her. "Good morning, Betty."

She looked up with a dazed expression, as if she was pulled out of a beautiful dream. "Oh, good morning, Grizzly, Ewan. I was just looking at a new video of little Emma."

Ewan suppressed a grin. Little Emma was Betty's first grandchild, and although the baby was so small that it didn't really do anything but sleep, Betty could watch videos of the tot all day long. She regularly shoved her phone under Ewan's nose, asking him whether this baby wasn't the most beautiful child ever, or whether he didn't see that Emma had Betty's nose. He didn't really see much besides a red-faced tiny human who didn't resemble any adult, but who looked like every baby did. But he didn't have the heart to tell Betty that. He always nodded and smiled and said she was the luckiest woman alive to be the grandmother of such a sweet little miracle.

"Where is Granny?" Grizzly asked.

"Where is Granny's mocha, you mean," Betty corrected him with a wink. "They can both be found in the conference room."

The conference room was a smaller space to

the right that was used as a meeting point for mountain rangers and a classroom where nature photographers taught people the ins and outs of focus and shutter time before going out into the wild to test their newly acquired skills. Sometimes tour groups had lunch there. But most often it was the spot where their team of paid workers and volunteers met up for a coffee, lemonade, snack and chat.

Grizzly rushed ahead of Ewan, throwing the door to the conference room open with a cry of joy. "I already smell what I'm after," he declared, heading straight for the table against the far wall where the coffee maker sat beside an assortment of cups and mugs.

"Won't you say good morning first?" Granny rebuked him. Short and slender, she looked like a fairy godmother from a storybook beside the giant man. But this fairy godmother didn't wear a sparkly dress but a red sweater and brown ripcord pants. Her boots were muddy, and there was a bloody scratch on her right hand.

Ewan walked over with a frown. Grizzly was pouring coffee while humming to himself. Ewan said to Granny, "What did you do?" He nodded at her hand. She looked down and frowned a moment as if the scratch didn't belong to her.

"I merely looked for a few items in the big barn." The big barn was a large brick building sitting a few yards back from the center. It harbored machinery and had a large attic full of boxes with items that could someday come in handy.

"I thought I had told you to ask me when you needed something. I don't mind going up in the attic to look."

"But you weren't here." Granny smiled up at him. "I may be seventy-five, but I can still climb a ladder and sort through a few boxes if I have to."

"That is the point," he insisted. "You don't have to. You could have asked Betty. She is twenty years younger."

"And terribly busy admiring the baby that has her nose." Granny winked. "I used to run this center with a lot less help and it always worked out."

He knew he would get her worked up if he kept repeating his point. Besides, he had to stay in her good graces to present his plan involving Gina Williams. He felt a jolt of nerves in his stomach—a sensation that was usually reserved for rescue missions. For the moments when he looked down from the helicopter as it closed in on the spot where he would be dropped, and he realized that the lives of the missing tourists might depend on him. On his ability to locate them before darkness set in or temperatures dropped below zero. He had done such missions often, but he never rested easy because of his prior successes. He knew, more than anyone else, that nature was unpredictable and nothing was a given. When his feet touched the ground as he slipped out of the chopper to start on his mission, he was fully aware that it was him against the elements and that he'd need all his knowledge and not a small dose of luck to accomplish what he came for. The mountains could be unforgiving of mistakes.

The same sense of urgency pressed on him now. There had been something about Gina Williams's response to her boss's news that had struck him as out of the ordinary. Yes, any employee who was suddenly told that their job ended would be shocked. Even upset because it hadn't been communicated earlier. They would wonder what the future held. But with Gina it had been different. She had responded like an animal to a predator. With dread. Fear for her survival.

He knew she was a widow with three small children. He didn't know when exactly her

husband had died, or under what circumstances. He just knew what he had seen in
her eyes. He assumed that she needed to make
money for her family and that her children's
future had been on her mind when Bud told
her the news. With spring also being a quiet
time in town, most businesses wouldn't be hir-
ing right now. She had a roof over her head at
her brother's ranch but he could imagine she
also wanted to contribute to the costs of living there. Pay for groceries, buy clothes and
toys for her children. If she loved her family
as he supposed she did, she wouldn't want to
burden them with her troubles.

He frowned. He hadn't grown up around
here so didn't have the deep insight into town
relations that most locals had. But he had
clearly sensed that finances were important
to her. She didn't want to end up jobless. And
he intended to help her with that.

Granny cleared her throat. "What is eating
you, Ewan? You have a frown a mile deep in
your forehead." She grinned at him. "Doesn't
make you look any younger."

"I don't mind my looks," Ewan said quickly,
casting a glance at Grizzly, who had filled the
biggest mug available with Granny's mocha
and had retreated to the window to look out

while he sipped. Ewan added in a low voice, "Could we, uh…discuss something privately?"

Granny raised an eyebrow at this request but waved him along through a door into the adjoining room where equipment was stored. She eyed him curiously. "If there's something I can help you with… For a change. It's usually you helping me." She crossed her arms over her chest. "It would make me feel better to do something in return."

Relief flooded Ewan. This was just the opening he needed. "Yes, there is something you can do for me. A real favor."

"I can't imagine, but tell me." She tilted her head with a skeptical gaze.

"The situation is like this. You know Bud Travers's Western store? In Heartmont? Well, I had to drop by there this morning to pick up some leather wax, and I overheard Bud talking about leaving town for a while. Closing up his business and all. It seems he's going to Texas for a bit to help a friend with a Western experience he has there."

Granny nodded. "And?"

"Well, he has this employee. A lady with a young family. A widow, sole provider for her kids. She's losing her job. She looked so upset and all, I thought um…she could come and work here. You know, help you out with the shop? She also makes apple products, delicious buns and pies that she could sell here."

Granny's expression changed from friendly and interested to guarded. "Look, Ewan, I know how you feel about me running the shop mostly on my own. You want me to accept help. Have said so for a long time. Now, is this business about me doing you a favor by taking on this widow a trick to lure me into accepting help? For if it is, I can tell you I am onto you. Onto you both. You must have told this woman all about me and…"

"Far from it. She knows next to nothing about the center and the shop here. She hasn't even visited since she was a little girl. I only want to help her find a new job now. It has nothing to do with you. I mean, with my earlier remarks about…" Ewan fell silent a moment. "It is not a trick," he ended meekly.

Granny studied him with a suspicious look. "If you say so."

"I suggested she drop by Saturday to have a look around and see what she thinks. She was reluctant, so I don't think I convinced her quite yet. I'll rely on your charm to do the rest."

"Ewan, I can't really…" Granny's frown deepened. "You are not the person to invite new people on board. I'm sorry to put it bluntly, but you like things to stay the way they are. You do well with our regular team so why rock the boat by inviting in a stranger? Someone who hasn't even visited the center recently. You know I'm usually quite critical when it comes to taking people on here. They have to feel a genuine connection to the mountains, to this environment and to the work we do here. This is not just *any* job. It requires enthusiasm. Tourists sense when you are not... engaged. How can you get them to appreciate the natural world unless you yourself are in love with it?"

"I'm sure she will do her best to learn fast. She has kids. She needs the job. Just give her a chance." It didn't sound like a well-rehearsed story, a convincing argument to get her on his side. But it seemed to work.

Granny's expression softened and she sighed. "If you put it like that..."

He relaxed just a little. Maybe he was halfway there.

Her sharp blue eyes searched his features. "Do you know this woman? I mean, have you met her before?"

"At the store, yes, but..."

"Aha."

The sound of those two syllables put the hairs on his neck on edge. What was she thinking? Like…he had an ulterior motive in inviting this woman to the center?

"This will be the day," Granny said softly, "where I find out Ewan McAllister isn't immune to female charm."

"It has nothing to do with… She was just helpless, you know? I wanted to help her. That is sort of what I do for a living. Helping people." He leaned over to her. "It's just a friendly gesture toward a fellow townsperson."

"Of course." Granny's expression went blank. "I understand. And I agree that she should be helped. That's what a community is for. Carry each other's burdens. Be there in a time of need. A widow, you said? Has she been alone long?"

"I don't know exactly."

"And children. How many?"

"Three. Two little girls and a baby boy."

"I see. That's quite a responsibility for a woman on her own."

"She's been living with her family for a while, on the Williams ranch. But I suppose she still has to earn her own keep. I mean, winter is a difficult season for any rancher."

"It certainly is."

"So her income from the job at Bud Travers's store could very well be important to her family as well. By letting her sell her products here you are helping her and her children, and her extended family." Ewan felt he was now really doing a great job at making his point. Once Gina visited, Granny would like her so much she'd have no reason not to want her to help out with the shop as well. He had to get Granny some help without her even noticing it was help.

Granny gave him a wide smile. "Why, Ewan, I have rarely seen you so involved with a local cause. I mean, you do a great job here at the center, but you are a...person who appreciates his own company over that of others. I hadn't expected you to be so...perceptive to a woman's needs."

Ewan had a feeling she was teasing him. He said quickly, "I guess it comes from always rescuing people. I just can't stop doing it." He shrugged. "But you will see she is a nice person, and her products are a good fit here. Just give it a chance."

"I'm already convinced." Granny put her hand on his arm. "Just don't let me discover later on that this was a setup to make me accept help. Just because I look like a nice little old lady doesn't mean I can't carry a grudge if you lie to me."

Ewan patted her hand and smiled, but inside he was just a little bit worried about Gina's visit on Saturday. After all, he had presented it to her as if Granny needed a lot of help. If Gina let that slip, there would be some explaining to do...

CHAPTER THREE

GINA PULLED THE rack from the oven and gave her apple cinnamon buns an appreciative look. They had a nice brown color and smelled delicious. Now just a little glaze to give them a good shine and they would be ready to deliver to Mrs. Beal for her birthday party this evening. It was a good thing she had this baking to do after her shift at the store had ended because otherwise her mind would circle nonstop on the big change in her life. A big change she hadn't been eager for. She bet lots of others were stuck in a rut and ached for an opportunity to start afresh. But she was a creature of habit and didn't like sudden disruptions to her daily routines.

"Mommy!" Stacey ran into the kitchen. Her honey-blond hair, pulled back in a ponytail, bobbed on her back. "Those smell so good. Can we taste them?"

"No, honey, these are for an order. I have

to deliver them. But I will bake cookies with you tonight. Okay? Cookies only take about twenty minutes to make. You can still try them before bed."

Stacey didn't seem convinced. "You always give the cookies to us, but we want to try something new and exciting. Like those buns."

Gina suppressed a laugh at her daughter's criticism. Still there was genuine disappointment in the girl's expression. She leaned down to wrap an arm around her. "Mommy thought up the recipe of the star cookies especially for you. Don't you remember?"

"Yes, you said we could make wishes. I wished you would be home more. You're always working."

A pang of guilt shot through Gina's chest. "Parents must work to provide for their children," she said quickly as if rehearsing a lesson from a book.

"Other children have a mommy and a daddy. If we had a daddy, he could put us to bed at night and read stories to us or do fun things with us while you work."

"You have a daddy, Stacey. He is in heaven."

"That's not much use. He can't do things with us. He can't talk to us." Stacey pulled away from Gina. "I'm going to feed the donkeys."

Gina wanted to say she had to wait for Grandma to go with her and help, but Stacey said, "I do know how," and ran off.

Gina sighed. At seven, her little girls were growing up more quickly than she wanted to acknowledge. They wanted to do things by themselves while she wanted to keep them close to her and...

Close to her, huh? Had Stacey not just blamed her for always working and not being there for them? Was she doing everything wrong, then? She thought it was right to work hard and save money and have some sort of independence. She dreamed of being able to afford her own house for the children and make it a real home. Not that this wasn't a real home but... It wasn't their home. It was her parents' ranch where she had received a very warm welcome during a hard time in her life but where she couldn't stay forever. Not if she took her responsibilities seriously.

"What is that delicious smell?" Lily came in and smiled at Gina. "I could have guessed it was you baking. Although your mom makes great sweet treats too. You must have inherited the baking gene from her." She crossed to the counter where the buns sat.

"They're for an order," Gina warned her.

Lily put her hands up in the air. "I wasn't going to touch them, just look at them. Do you need help delivering them? It's no trouble for me to do it. Then you can cook dinner with the girls."

Gina gave her a closer look. "Did you over-hear what Stacey said to me?" That was the trouble living under the same roof with your extended family. Everyone knew everything. It was okay most of the time, but sometimes it felt like she had no privacy. No way to raise her family the way she wanted without others having an opinion about it.

It made her insecure sometimes.

"She bumped into me and said something about you always being busy for other people." Lily flashed an apologetic smile. "It isn't true, of course, but a girl her age doesn't see it that way. She likes to exaggerate. Also to get at-tention I guess."

"Attention she deserves to get." Gina sighed. "She said to me that other kids have a father and a mother. Two people to care for them, listen to them, spend time with them. It re-minded me that I have to do twice the work. And maybe I am not doing it."

"Gina…" Lily stepped up to her and gave her a hug. "Please don't feel that way. You are doing a marvelous job. You take such good care of your children. Provide for them by working hard at the store. Creating sweet treats to have even more money to spend on their wants and needs. They don't miss anything."

"Yes, they do. They miss their father."

Lily held Gina's gaze. "You didn't take him away from them. It's not your fault."

"No, but I do have to make up for what they miss. And sometimes it feels like I have to keep so many plates spinning that I'm bound to fail. I just can't do it all by myself."

"Nobody says you should. We're all here to help. Let me deliver the buns and you can cook with the girls." Lily squeezed her arm. "Once Stacey is laughing again, you will also feel better."

"Lily…" Gina swallowed hard. "How can I ever feel better when Barry is dead? He is not coming back. Ever."

Lily held her gaze. Hurt flashed in her eyes and Gina felt immediately guilty. Barry was Lily's brother. She also missed him. "I'm sorry," she said hurriedly. "I shouldn't have said that. You're right. Stacey will soon feel better. It's just a little girl's bad mood. It will pass."

Lily said, "You never said it quite like that before. You're always trying to be cheerful and telling all of us it's going okay. But if you really feel that way, deep down inside…"

"It's nothing." Gina rushed to find ways to assure Lily there was really nothing amiss. "I'm just having a very difficult day. Bud fired me."

"What?"

As she had hoped, this crudely put announcement distracted Lily at once. "He fired you?" she echoed in a tone of utmost disbelief. "How is that possible? For what? You're always doing what he wants, coming early, staying late… Cade said last week he was taking advantage of you, and Mom agreed."

Gina said, "Well, he did fire me. Not because of anything I did wrong but because he's closing the business."

"What?" Now Lily looked even more shocked. "Is he bankrupt? Oh, I'm so sorry for you, Gina. I know how hard this must have hit you. Such bad news and…"

"He decided, for his own reasons, to close the store for a few months. He's not bankrupt, although I don't know if he won't be later this year, acting so irresponsible for a man his age. Imagine this." She spread her arms in a dramatic wide gesture. "He's packing up and moving to Texas for a while to help a friend run a Western experience. It has always been his dream, he said. Yeah, well, it's well and good to have dreams, but you can't just run after them and drop everything else, you know."

"That doesn't sound like him at all," Lily marveled.

"Well, he made a sign, and he will put it on the shop door on Friday when he closes up. I took a photo because I figured none of you would believe it." Gina got her phone from the nearby table and held it out to Lily, who studied the photo with raised eyebrows.

"Wow. It must be true, then. Still… I almost think he was pulling your leg. Are you sure he's leaving town?"

"One hundred percent sure. And that means I have no more job."

Lily looked up with a start. "Oh, but you will find something new in no time. I'm sure Cade can ask around and…"

Gina felt her heart clench a moment at the idea that her brother would go to his town contacts to beg them for a job for her. Of course, he would mean well, and everyone in town had been so nice when she had arrived with the children and two suitcases and a mountain of debt, but…it wasn't like that anymore. She was rebuilding her life, and she needed to do this her way.

"Don't you worry. I already have another job."

Lily tilted her head. "Honestly? Or are you just saying that so I don't worry?"

She thinks I can't handle my life. She feels like I need to be watched over and taken care of and... She means well, but it isn't right. I am a mother of three. I need to be able to take care of my own family.

"Yes, I mean it. You know the tourist information center in Hillock? It has a shop where they sell products to tourists. I can sell my baked goods there." She hadn't even decided yet that she was going to, but she had to convince Lily that it was all taken care of. That she had a new job waiting for her and they need not worry. What had Ewan also said? That she could help out on busier days? Weekends, spring break. And even more in the summer. She added boldly, "I can also help selling stuff and doing chores. It's a regular job. It's all arranged for. I'm going there Saturday to meet everyone. The other workers and my new boss, Mrs. Grant. I heard she is a fantastic elderly lady."

"But Gina…" Lily stood motionless as if she had trouble processing all of that. "You hate mountains. You never want to go anywhere near them. You always say it reminds you of…"

The way Barry died. Yes. Her throat constricted a moment. "That was earlier. It's been two years now. I'm over that. I mean, it is just silly to cling to such an idea. The mountains here have absolutely nothing to do with what happened."

Lily came closer and reached out a hand. "Gina, I don't want you to do something you don't want to just because you lost your job with Bud. Like I said, Cade can ask around and…"

"I already agreed to go and look at the center, meet the people. It was meant to be that that man was in the store just when Bud told me the news. He works in Hillock. He'll show us around on Saturday. I'll take the kids. They deserve a day out. He has a dog they'll love."

Lily blinked. "You're going to the Rockies with the kids? But you never wanted them near mountains. You always say it will make them sad again. Or bring up new questions about how Barry—"

"I couldn't let this opportunity pass," Gina rushed to say. "It was just too good. Besides, that man was really kind to offer it. I didn't want to hurt his feelings."

"It would be better to hurt a perfect stranger's feelings than to put yourself through this confrontation with an environment you hate."

"Lily, please, it's alright. I'll glaze these and then you can deliver them." Gina was happy Lily had offered to do it so she could get her away. She hugely appreciated her sister-in-law and all she had done for them so far, but this was her own decision.

Lily looked doubtful but retreated to go and get her jacket and purse. Gina quickly mixed the glaze. She forced herself to pay attention so it didn't get too thin and ruin the buns. Her baking brought in money, and she had a reputation to guard. Soon her treats would be sold at the tourist information center.

She remembered it only vaguely. Walking in with Dad's hand around hers, looking at the mounted animals together. They had been majestic and so lifelike. She had sometimes worried they could suddenly move, snap at her. Dad had squeezed her hand to reassure her, or even lifted her into his arms. She had felt so safe then. So loved.

Gina swallowed hard. If only Dad were alive, to wink at her and tell her she was doing a good job as a mother. That her kids would be fine despite missing their daddy.

They missed their daddy. Just as she missed her Dad.

Gina blinked furiously against the burn behind her eyes. She didn't want to keep feeling this. Like she had just told Lily, it had been two years since the avalanche had snatched Barry away. And Dad had died a good ten years before that. It was so long ago she should be able to move on. But still, at the most unexpected moments, she missed him. She wished she could talk to him. Or just hide in his arms. Dad had always understood her without words. He had known how to reach her even if she didn't want to listen. He…

You make him sound like a saint, she scolded herself, still fighting the tears. *He never liked talking and that was sometimes hard. You didn't always see eye to eye. You moved away and married and built your own life.*

And still…

Couldn't she understand her little girl aching for her daddy? If she, a grown woman, still missed her father so much…

Maybe she should have told her that instead of reasoning with her. Trying to remove her sadness with nice words.

But Gina knew that if she allowed herself to feel the pain she would break down and cry in front of her children, and that would just upset them. They needed security. They had that when she was strong. She needed to be calm and unemotional, for the sake of all of them. For Stacey. For Ann, who would not say what she was thinking. And for little Barry, a cheerful boy who hadn't known his father and didn't really miss him because he didn't know what to miss.

She wiped the back of her hand across her eyes quickly, took a deep breath. She had buns to pack and then dinner to cook. Lily would probably take the news about her new job straight to Cade and maybe even to Mom. To get them on her side and form a united front to talk her out of trying at the center? She didn't know what to expect really. Her entire world had been turned upside down today, and at the center of the chaos was a man who had thrown her a lifeline. At least she had seen it that way when she had grabbed it. Now she was starting to doubt the wisdom of her decision. How could she know what to do? When she had still worked at the pizzeria, had put all her energy into the business that was Barry's and hers, she had believed in her own abilities. She had thought up fun promotions and had interacted with the customers. And when they were happy, she had been happy as well.

But the debts had wiped everything away and... It had made her feel like a total failure. Someone who should never have gone into business to begin with. Maybe she was just not cut out for it.

Those doubts now assailed her anew. What was she doing? How would she manage?

Especially with her family not being fully supportive of the plan. Why take such chances?

But she had just told Lily that she was going on Saturday, so she had to. Whether she believed in herself or not.

CHAPTER FOUR

LILY PUT THE glazed buns in the back of her car and shut the door. Then she glanced in the direction of the big barn where the animals were housed. Would Cade be in there? She longed to see him for a moment before she left. She checked her watch and decided she did have a minute to spare. With a thrill of excitement in her chest, she ran the few paces to the barn door and opened it carefully.

Inside it was a little dim, and her eyes took time to adjust. She heard the familiar sounds of the animals scurrying, and the scent of hay rose in her nose. This place felt like a safe haven, away from the rest of the world, where she could come to cuddle her furry friends and find a few moments of peace in an otherwise full day. On a ranch like theirs there was always work to do in the orchard and around the house. They also had to take things to town and meet up with people. Cade was involved with several local initiatives, and after their wedding Lily had naturally found her way into joining as well, whether it was supporting fundraising for a playground at the school or starting a book club. Two years ago when she had still lived in the city, chasing a career in advertising and promotion, she would never have seen herself in a small town, let alone on a ranch. She had loved animals, for sure, and she had loved working at the communal garden project where she could get her hands dirty and grow her own vegetables. But she had never seen herself as a country girl. Her dreams had consisted of work-related goals. Now it was all relationship goals. Growing in her marriage with Cade, being part of his family and the community. Helping new friends.

Lily took a deep breath of the sweet-scented air. This was such a good life. She had fully embraced it and was completely happy here. So lucky to have found this place and this man.

Her husband.

She smiled as she looked at Cade, who was brushing one of their donkeys. Mollie and Millie had come to the ranch when Gina had come to live here with her girls. At the time she had been pregnant with little Barry. Now he was a bouncy little boy of eighteen months. How time flew by.

Cade looked up and spotted her. A smile lit up his features. "Hey, you there."

"Hey, yourself." Lily closed in. "I'm going to drive out for a bit to deliver some buns for Gina. They are for a birthday party tonight. She just finished them, and she has to cook dinner with the girls so... I thought I could do it. Let her spend time with Stacey and Ann for a bit. It seems Stacey feels a little ignored."

"How come?" Cade asked, a frown furrowing his brow. "We're all here to look after them. Mom spends a lot of time with them, teaching them how to knit and crochet. I'm glad winter is over because we'd all be adorned top to bottom with woolen items soon."

Lily laughed. "Poor you."

But Cade looked serious as he stepped out of the enclosure and shut the door. His gaze was pensive as he continued, "I try to have time for them every day, even though there is always so much work to do. But we play games and you read them stories if they want to. How is it possible she feels like we don't give her enough attention?"

"I don't know. But she told Gina that other

kids have two parents and she only has a mommy. Not a daddy."

Cade's jaw clenched.

Lily reached out and put her hand on his arm. "Don't be hard on yourself, Cade. You do what you can. We all do. But we can't replace their father. If they miss having a daddy, we must accept that. Respect that that is the way they feel. They may be young, but they do have a lot of feelings about it."

Cade nodded. "I know. I guess that I had this simplistic idea that if we took them in and showered them with love, baked cakes and gave them guinea pigs, they would forget the heartbreak and be happy again. As if you can cover hurt with candy. I'm sorry that I felt that way."

"No. I totally understand. You just wanted them to stop crying and laugh again like children should. I guess most of the time they are happy. At least they're safe here. They have a stable home, a place where they can relax and play and be with people who love them. That's the most important thing." Lily's heart skipped a beat thinking of the news Gina had shared with her. That she was now jobless. It wouldn't be easy for her to find something new at short notice…though it seemed she already had.

Cade studied her features. "What is it? I can always see it when you think of a problem. There's this shadow that crosses your face."

Lily looked down. "It's nothing really." She had come in here for a moment to see Cade and think of how happy he made her. Not to burden him with something. Gina had to be the one to tell him anyway.

Cade put his hand under her chin and lifted her face to him. "Come on, Lily, I know there is something. Just tell me. Maybe I can help?"

Lily sighed. "It's not really my place to tell you. Gina should."

"Does it have to do with Gina? Is something the matter? Is she ill?" He sounded worried, his blue eyes darkening like the summer skies when a sudden storm pulled in.

Lily shook her head. "There's nothing wrong with her personally. It's about her work situation. With Bud Travers."

"I see. I know Bud can be a handful, but Gina must try and work with him as best she can. That job means a lot to her. I know she is doing the baking stuff and maybe thinking about earning more money that way, but it's way too uncertain. She needs a steady day job. For her future and for the kids' sake."

Lily studied his expression. "I think it's

wonderful she loves baking so much and that her products are wanted around town."

"Yes, me too, but..."

Before he could protest that it was more of a hobby, and it should stay that way, Lily said, "That is just what I'm saying. We're thinking the same thing, Cade, don't worry."

He held her gaze a moment, ready to argue, it seemed, and then suddenly a smile broke the tension in his features. "That's good," he said slowly. He reached out to brush his fingers down her cheek. "It's good that we are agreed on it, because I don't want us to disagree about anything."

Lily's heart leaped with joy under his tender touch. That look in his eyes... She had never known that a man could actually look at a woman like that. How good it felt to be so loved. She stood on tiptoe to put her lips to his. For a brief moment she fell into the warmth that had overtaken her from the first moment she had met Cade, here on the ranch. The warmth and the sense of belonging. She had found a home here.

Cade deepened the kiss, pulling her into his embrace. Lily closed her eyes, and she could forget all the difficult questions about Gina's situation, Stacey's unhappiness, the future,

near and far. She was here with the man she
loved, and all was well.

Then she pulled her head away and said
breathlessly, "I have that delivery to do, Cade.
And I bet you weren't done with the animals
either."

Cade grinned. "They can wait."

"But Mrs. Beal can't. If she starts calling
Gina to ask where her buns are…"

Cade sighed. "Okay, if you have to go." He
kissed her quickly. "Hurry back."

GINA KEPT HER eye on the door into the big barn.
What was Lily doing in there? Instead of stepping into her car and driving off to get that delivery to Mrs. Beal right away, she had gone
into the barn and still hadn't come back out
again.

Was Cade there? Were they discussing her
situation? The fact that she was out of a job
now and completely dependent on them again?

The idea was painful. It was probably just
her imagination. She knew Lily would never
see her as a burden.

Her rational mind knew that, at least. Her
feelings were a whole different matter. A mess
of tangled fear, anxiety, doubt, worries…

At last, the door opened and Lily stepped

out. Cade followed her and blew kisses after her. He stood at the door with a wide grin on his face, watching Lily as she got into her car. Then he waved while she drove off. Her big brother, a no-nonsense man, acting like a loved-up teen.

That was what love did to people. It opened them up to the sun. They suddenly felt things they hadn't felt before.

Gina wished she could still feel those things. That it wasn't so very cold inside her. So cold and rigid. As if she had to stand up straight like she was in a school camp with a very strict leader who came to inspect her every morning. Checked if she was wide awake, freshly washed and dressed, if all her buttons were done up correctly. She wanted to be a picture of perfection. She was a mother after all, who wanted to take good care of her children. Her household had to run smoothly and…

A hissing sound behind her back made her jerk around. The water she had put on for soup was boiling over. She ran to the stove, grabbed an oven mitt and pulled the pan off the element. So much for the perfect mother she wanted to be. At least boiling water didn't make a mess like plenty of other things did.

"Can I lend you a hand?" Mom had come in and smiled at her.

Gina felt a little caught out. As a girl she had often tried to cook for the family and made a mess of it, with her mother gently guiding her back onto the right path. She felt a little like that now.

"I'm just making some soup. I wanted the girls to help me with the vegetables and the meatballs. Where are they?"

"Stacey is in the hallway with her skipping rope. Ann is in her room doing something with a lot of pink glitter." Mom grinned. "I don't think they are very eager to drop everything and come to help you."

"I wanted to cook together to have some time for the girls. With all my baking lately, I feel like I'm neglecting them."

"Oh." Mom came to stand beside her, leaning against the sink. "I had the impression baking makes you happy. I've been hearing you singing and humming like never before."

A pang of guilt hit Gina. She had been singing and humming, feeling almost…happy? That would be terrible. How could she be happy while her husband had died and her children were growing up without a father?

Happy was totally the wrong word. *Content*

was more like it. She appreciated what she did have. That was different from being happy. Mom shouldn't get the wrong impression. "I can do something I'm good at and make money with it for my family. That's a reason to be grateful."

Mom nodded. She waited a moment and then said, "You don't have to excuse yourself for being glad sometimes, Gina."

Gina blinked at her. Her mind seemed to stop processing a moment. It wasn't wrong to be happy? Of course it was wrong. Before Barry had died, she hadn't seen the danger lurking to snatch her happiness away. Barry had handled all their finances. She had known almost nothing about expenses, bills, fees. She had fully trusted him, but still…hadn't her ignorance been kind of naive? What kind of businesswoman and partner had she been, not knowing what was going on until it was too late? Until her children had been homeless.

How could she ever forget that? *She* had let that all happen. She hadn't been able to prevent it. Or stop it. Turn it around. She had disappointed so many people.

Mom said, "You have a lot to be glad about. The girls are healthy, little Barry is growing up fine and we have a good life here, together. Why wouldn't you hum and sing?"

"I guess that…sometimes I feel I'm having it a little too easy." Gina nodded slowly as she went to the fridge to look for vegetables for the soup. "Like it shouldn't be like this, you know." She opened the door and peered inside without really registering what was there. "Other widows are alone in the world, having to fend for their families singlehanded. I have so much help and… Maybe I should do more. On my own."

As she said it, she cringed. Why did she have to be so honest? Mom wouldn't understand. Would jump at her with reasons why it was fine the way it was. After all, she enjoyed having her grandchildren around her.

But her mom remained silent. Gina tried to think of what she needed for the soup. Reluctantly she selected some carrots and a package of ground beef. Tension was building in the silence. She almost wanted to turn around and shout, "Just say it. Say that I should be grateful for all I have here and not long for my own life. My own household, my own family to take care of without others interfering. It's not that I don't love you, because I do, but… sometimes… I think of the past and I wish…"

She closed the door and carried the carrots and ground beef to the sink. "I'm sorry, Mom. It's been a long, hard day. Bud Travers is closing up the store. He told me that I'm no longer needed there."

It was the perfect bombshell news to distract Mom from what she had said. To avoid a real conversation about what was bothering her.

As expected, her mother gasped and said, "What? Closing the store? But I thought he was always making a decent living off it. Why would he suddenly close it?"

"He is moving to Texas where a buddy has a Western experience. He wants to help him. Allegedly for a few months, but… You know how those things go. Before he knows it, he'll be all settled in there and not wanting to come back here. He loves Western stuff, and he is a man on his own, so he can move away if he wants to. Doesn't have to take other people's opinions into account."

Mom nodded slowly. "I guess you're right. But, it is rather sudden. When is he closing the store?"

"Friday is the last day open. Saturday he will be in Texas."

"I never thought he was a man to make such impulsive decisions." Mom paced the kitchen.

"Or that he would let you down like that. I mean it's all good and fine for him to jump into an adventure like that, but he can't just give you notice and turn you out in a few days' time."

Gina shrugged. "Well, he did. He said he'd pay my salary in full for this entire month. So I won't be losing money. I mean, I…" *Will just be losing my job.* She grabbed a knife and started to clean the carrots.

Mom said, "How did you take it?"

"I didn't break down and cry." Gina grabbed the knife tighter and chopped a carrot into small bits. "I was shocked, but…" Still, hadn't she shown some emotion? Maybe not tears but panic? After all, Ewan McAllister, who had just come in to buy something, had sensed her mood right away.

Men were usually not that sensitive to feelings. At least, in her experience a woman had to be pretty obvious about what she felt before they caught on. But Ewan seemed to be different.

Mom said, "Look, Gina, there is nothing wrong with being upset about getting fired. Especially as it isn't your fault. You didn't do anything to cause this. You were never late. You always did what he asked you to do."

That was probably what made it feel so unfair, Gina thought. She had worked hard to please him and ensure he kept her on and now he was just walking away.

She bit her lip. This feeling of being left out to dry was painfully familiar. After Barry had died, she had lain awake at night and clenched her hands into fists and silently shouted at him: Why did you have to go on the skiing trip? Why were your friends more important than your family? Why did you have to go where there could be avalanches? Why did you take so much risk while I was pregnant with your son?

She had never found answers. And she had even blamed herself for her anger. Barry had died in an accident. He and his friends had been on a route that was generally considered safe. They hadn't done anything irresponsible. His friends had felt terrible that Barry had died while they had all survived. She could still see their pale anxious faces on the day of his funeral. No, it had just been one of those unfortunate occurrences in life. Something you couldn't understand no matter how long or hard you thought about it.

Mom said softly, "You shouldn't blame Bud. He probably figures at his age he must take the opportunities that are offered to him. And like you said, he has no one to consider. He can do whatever he wants."

She nodded. "I know. I understand. And it doesn't matter all that much as I already have another job. I mean, on Saturday I'm going to see a place where I can work."

Mom blinked in surprise.

A strange sense of excitement trickled through Gina's chest. She didn't have to depend on them to cheer her up or find her a way out. No. She had a solution at hand, something she'd worked out by herself. Well, something she'd been offered by Ewan. But she could shape this new chance for herself. Without needing to lean on her family to help her out. They had already done enough for her. She had to repay their faith in her by showing that she could make it.

"You know the tourist information center in Hillock? It seems the elderly lady who runs the gift shop there is short a pair of hands. And not only can I work there, I can also sell my baking."

"Oh, that sounds great. Did Bud set this up for you?"

"Why would you think so?" Gina's enthusiasm deflated in an instant. Her mother immediately assumed someone else had solved the issue for her. Probably because that was what everybody had been doing ever since she had come to live here. Making sure her life ran smoothly.

"Oh, I thought that maybe to sweeten the disappointment he offered…"

"No. This is something I arranged for myself." Gina straightened up. "I'll go and get Stacey. She wanted to spend time with me, so now she can help me make soup." She walked into the hallway where Stacey was skipping. "Come and make soup with me," she invited.

"I can't now," Stacey said, her breathing uneven because of the exertion. "I'm going to skip…a hundred times. I am at seventy-five."

"You wanted to do something together. I'm making soup especially for you."

"I don't want to now." Stacey was counting under her breath. "Ask Ann."

"Ann is crafting."

"I am skipping."

"You asked me to spend more time with you."

"Mom, I'm losing count. Just go away."

Stacey jumped two more times, then her left leg got caught in the rope. She almost fell over. Gina reached out to catch her, but Stacey brushed her off. "I can manage. Now I didn't make a hundred times and have to start all over."

"Some other time. You're panting. Come into the kitchen with me."

"You're not asking Ann to stop crafting."

Gina took a deep breath to argue, but Stacey said, "Oh well, if I have to." She threw her skipping rope on the floor and walked to the kitchen, head down, shoulders slumped.

Automatically, Gina reached down to pick up the rope and put it away so no one would trip over it. She didn't understand her daughter at all. One moment she was practically begging her for attention, now she wanted to be left alone? For a game of skip rope?

In the kitchen Mom had fetched the step stool so Stacey could reach the sink. She unwrapped the ground beef and told her to make nice balls, all the same size. "Else they won't all be cooked inside when they land on our plates."

Stacey laughed and rubbed her head over Mom's shoulder.

Gina took a deep breath. A few moments before, Stacey had been bursting with frustration, and now she seemed carefree and happy to oblige.

Maybe Mom was just the better educator? Maybe Gina didn't have a clue what she was doing?

She knew this assessment was probably unfair, but after a long day of work at the store, baking and parenting, she wasn't in the mood to be very reasonable. Her phone beeped and she pulled it out of her pocket. Mrs. Beal maybe about the buns? What if she didn't like them?

But it was a message from Ewan. She had messaged him earlier to say she was coming Saturday, and was bringing the girls. He now sent a photo of himself posing beside a giant mounted bear with the words *We can bearly wait*.

Gina laughed softly. She had noticed in the store that he was tall, but now she realized he was almost as tall as that bear. Next to a giant predator like that some people might look small, but Ewan cut a good figure. He looked like the sort of guy you could depend on to find the way in the mountains. To get you safely from A to B.

He looked sporty too. Probably liked outdoor activities. Hiking, cycling, canoeing.

Skiing? a small voice in the back of her head asked.

Her hand tensed on the phone. The center was in mountainous terrain. She knew that. She had decided it didn't matter, but didn't it really? What if Ewan loved skiing? What if he talked about it to the girls and they would get upset about Daddy?

Gina bit her lip and put the phone away. She was reasoning about the girls, but didn't she really mean herself? Wouldn't she get upset if she was confronted with such an environment? A place that reminded her so much of how Barry had died?

She could have gone anywhere to work. A restaurant. A clothes boutique. A bookshop. A library. Places that were worlds away from the snow that had claimed Barry's life. From the sort of activities that Barry had loved and gone after rather than staying home with the people who needed him.

"Was that Mrs. Beal?" Mom asked. "Is she happy with her buns?"

"Yes. No. Um…"

"Isn't she happy?" Mom tilted her head. "Your buns are delicious."

"No, it wasn't Mrs. Beal. It was…someone from the book club. I'll call her later."

Gina crossed to Stacey and put a hand on her shoulder. "I'm sorry that I broke your attempt to skip a hundred times. I bet you would have been very proud of yourself if you had made it."

Stacey looked up at her. "I want to be strong like Daddy. He could skip a thousand times."

Barry had also used a skipping rope for conditioning. The girls had thought it very funny as most daddies didn't do any such thing.

"You know what?" She brushed the girl's hair back. "Saturday we are going to do something fun. All of us. You, me, Ann and little Barry. We're going to a place you have never been before."

Stacey squealed. "The big indoor playground? The one that was in the paper?"

Gina shook her head. That playground charged an extravagant entrance fee. Too expensive for a family outing. "No. It's not a playground. Guess again."

"If it's not a playground…" Stacey looked disappointed. "It's not about crafting, is it? Crafting is boring."

"No. It's something very exciting. With animals."

"The zoo! We are going to the zoo." Stacey jumped off the step and danced through the kitchen.

Gina's heart sank. She should never have

let her daughter guess. Now she was coming up with all these options out of reach. A zoo charged even more than the indoor playground. She couldn't afford anything like that.

"It's not a zoo." She took out her phone and pulled up the photo of Ewan with the bear. "Here, have a peek. But don't tell Ann yet."

As expected, Stacey jumped at the chance to know something her sister wasn't to know just yet. She ran to her mother and looked at the photo on the screen. "Is that a bear?" There was awe in her voice. "Did he kill the bear?"

"No, I'm sure he didn't kill the bear. The bear is there for kids to learn about wild animals. Then we can go outside and see the woods."

"Oh. Are there any live bears there? I'd love to see a wild bear."

"I don't think so." Gina shuddered at the idea of her little girl running into a bear. She had to ask Ewan about that. If it was in any way dangerous, they weren't going. At all.

"Not a word to Ann," she warned Stacey and then said to her mother, "Can you supervise the cooking for a minute? I need to make a call." Leaving the kitchen, she went to her bedroom. She sat down on her bed and took a deep breath, then called Ewan. He answered on the third ring. "Hello?"

"Ewan, this is Gina. Thanks for the lovely photo. It got my little girl all worked up. She wants to see real bears. But, um… I'm a little bit worried about that. There aren't any bears there, right? I mean, not where they can get near my girls."

"No, sometimes there's a bear in the region, but they never get near the center. The rangers keep an eye out for tracks and make sure there isn't any food left that might attract bears. We educate tourists to take their trash back to the center and not dump it along the paths. Food really is the thing that can get them interested. Otherwise, they avoid getting too close to humans."

"Okay. I guess it was rather silly of me to think a bear could just come and… Then again, I don't know all that much about the place where you work. So I will really need to depend on you to, uh…" *Keep us safe?* "Teach us more."

"I'd be happy to. No, Fuzzy, that is *not* your dinner…"

She suppressed a laugh. Ewan said apologetically, "Fuzzy thinks I shouldn't be chatting but giving her her food. To ensure that I get the message, she is now trying to get to my steak. She's small, but you'd be surprised how clever she is about getting to things when she really wants them."

"I can imagine. The kids have been begging me for their own dog for ages. We have a dog here, Rosie, a border collie, that belongs to my mom and brother. She's the ranch's guard dog and a very clever girl. But she isn't ours, you know. We do have donkeys and guinea pigs and other animals we rescued."

"Oh, that's great. Tell me more."

"We rescued them when we still lived in the city. We had a communal garden project there with a shed attached where we kept the rescues. Everyone pitched in to care for them. My girls are especially fond of the donkeys because they have such floppy ears."

"So we have something in common. We rescue animals. Well, I say, *animals* plural, but I've only rescued one little dog. I think I need to learn more about rescuing other animals. Bigger ones."

It was sort of sweet to imagine he might not have been around animals much in his life. Maybe he grew up in the city. In an apartment building where they didn't allow pets. Maybe he was happy he now finally had the dog he had always wanted as a kid.

She caught herself smiling again. There was

something about Ewan that evoked a feeling she hadn't had in a long time. A sort of...tenderness?

A knock on her door jerked her away from the bed. She clenched the phone as if caught red-handed. "Um, I have to go. My dinner is on the stove. Talk to you later."

"I look forward to it."

Gina held the phone behind her back as she called, "Come in."

Mom peeked around the door. "Stacey is ready with the meatballs. What else do you want in your soup?"

Mom, you can make soup without me. Gina felt like her mother had wanted to know whom she was calling. Maybe that was her own fault because she had been kind of secretive about the earlier message. Why had she lied about whom the sender was? She might be living at home again, but she wasn't a teenager anymore. If she believed in this new venture, she should show it, back her own choice.

She followed her mother to the kitchen. Stacey stood at the sink, her hands sticky from the meatballs. Ann stood opposite her, holding out her hands covered in pink glitter. "I just want to wash my hands," she said primly, "without having to guess where we are going on Saturday."

"Let Ann use the tap, Stacey," Mom said gently but firmly.

Stacey sighed and made way. While Ann washed her hands, Stacey looked at Gina. "I haven't told her yet. But I really want to. Can I?"

As Gina hesitated, Stacey shouted, "Please, Mommy, please?"

"Okay. But…" *Do it gently, don't go mentioning giant bears.*

"We're going to see a man who has a bear." Stacey stared at Ann with wide-open eyes to emphasize the thrill.

"A bear?" Ann squeaked. "A real bear?"

"Yes, and it's bigger than him. It has claws and it does…" Stacey held up her hands with bent fingers and made growling noises as she moved toward Ann. Ann screamed and scurried back. She held up the hand towel as if it could be a shield to protect her. "You're lying. No one has a bear like that."

"He does. I saw a photo." Stacey growled even more and grabbed with her dirty fingers at Ann.

Ann hid behind Gina. "I don't want to go. I don't have to go, do I, Mommy? I don't want to." She pushed her face against Gina's back. "I don't want to. I'll cry if I have to."

"You're afraid of everything," Stacey said with disgust.

"Girls…" Gina's mother shook her head. "Try and be nice to each other. Stacey, wash your hands now." Turning to Ann, she leaned down and said softly, "There is no dangerous animal there, Ann. Your mommy surely wouldn't take you to a dangerous place. You know that."

Gina's heart clenched. Was it dangerous there? How did she know? She hadn't gone there alone first to make sure. How could she make her girls feel safe? She could, of course, keep them close to her. She would stay far away from anything risky, so with her near, the girls had to be safe as well. Had to be.

Still, her breathing quickened as if she had run a long way. She was doing something new and potentially risky, and it didn't feel right. She wished for a moment she could change her mind, tell Ewan she wouldn't be coming.

But she couldn't. She had promised Ewan. Besides, she needed the job. She needed the chance to sell her baking away from Heartmont. If this became a success she might… start her own business?

That would be way riskier than going to a tourist information center near mountains. It would be an outright threat to her financial stability. How could she even think about it? She had children to raise. Three of them, no less.

She went to the playpen where little Barry was sitting quietly playing with his cars. Where the girls were very vocal and always clamoring for her attention, he was content being by himself, exploring the world around him with tentative fingers. He liked to look carefully before he decided how he felt about things. He may have Barry's eyes, but his nature was a lot like hers.

She picked him up and cuddled him. She stood there, cradling her little boy in her arms while she watched her mother rally the girls into setting the table. The cooking soup spread a delicious smell. It needed more ingredients, but the start was there.

Her start was here as well. She was going to see Ewan on Saturday and explore what the center might mean for her business opportunities. She had to go and do it, or she'd regret it forever.

She kissed her little boy on the cheek. He cooed and cuddled against her. He was the living reminder of the man she had loved. In this child, Barry would always be with her, be part of her life. But it was also time to move on and find a way to make her family work on her own. Spreading her wings bit by bit. It was scary, and she wasn't even sure she could make it. She didn't know if her family would approve or feel she was rocking the boat for no reason, disappointing them. She saw obstacles all around.

But she also knew she had to try. Because just thinking about having her own business, making her baking and cooking not just a hobby but so much more, gave her joy she had never imagined feeling after Barry had died. It lit up her life. She couldn't let it slip away. She had to guard every smile that she found inside herself like her hands guarding a flame against an ice-cold wind. That flame had to keep burning. It had to keep her warm.

CHAPTER FIVE

EWAN REACHED UP a moment to check the collar of his shirt. He was never very particular about how he dressed when he went to the center to show people around, but this Saturday was different. Gina was coming with her little family. He wanted her to have a good impression of him and the location. He knew she'd care about that. She seemed to worry a lot. Something that was understandable in her position. She had the full responsibility for her children. No partner to share the weight with, to discuss things. He admired her for all that she did. She had to be a very strong woman with a kind heart. The way in which she had immediately reached out to the frightened little rescue dog…

He smiled down on Fuzzy, who sat beside him, her wagging tail dusting the floorboards. It seemed she had caught on to his excitement and knew it was a special day. That they were here waiting for some very special people.

"Aren't they here yet?" Granny asked, popping up beside him. Her eyes surveyed him with interest as she added, "You have been on the lookout for half an hour."

He suppressed the urge to rub his neck, something he always did when uncomfortable. "Look, I just want them to feel welcome. Gina had a shock when she lost her job earlier this week and… But better not mention that. I don't want her to feel like she can only sell her products here because we feel sorry for her."

"Oh, I wouldn't dream of that. I hate people who feel sorry for me. Think I can't do things because I am old and frail." Granny raised an expressive eyebrow before retreating to the shop area.

The hot and itchy feeling on Ewan's neck increased. He had gotten himself into a nice jam. To get Gina to come here he had made Granny seem like more of a helpless old lady than she really was. But if Gina let on, Granny would be outraged and take it out on him first chance she got. He could take the heat, but he was a little worried it would set Granny's mind against Gina as an unwelcome newcomer who was invading her space. That would be a bad start to the whole undertaking.

Oh wait. Was that them? He watched as the

SUV turned into the yard. It was a big enough car to hold a few kids and her baked goods. His heart beat fast and his focus became laser sharp as it was during rescue missions. He took in every detail: the license number, the way the door stuck a moment before opening, the little girl that clambered out first. She had blond hair pulled back in a ponytail and wore blue coveralls over a yellow T-shirt. She pulled a small backpack out after her. She seemed to shout something into the car.

Now the driver's door opened and Gina got out. The sun lit her hair, outlined her posture as she stood a moment leaning down to the little girl to straighten her ponytail. His breath caught as he watched the intimacy of that little scene. Her gesture was so natural, something she did probably without thought. The little girl looked up at her and he saw the resemblance in their features. Would this be Stacey or Ann? As they were twins, would he even be able to tell them apart? He had a feeling he would make a bad impression if he couldn't.

The girl wanted to run away, but Gina seemed to tell her to wait. She stood impatiently skipping from one foot to the other, her eyes taking in everything around her. In the sky a bird of prey cried out and immediately she looked up. It made him smile. It would be easy to teach such a perceptive little girl about the joys of nature.

Now a second girl clambered from the car. She seemed reluctant to leave it and stood close to it, looking around with a forlorn expression. She also wore coveralls and had a blond ponytail, but her T-shirt was red.

Thank you, Gina, for making this easier on me.

Fuzzy whined and pulled at the leash, clearly wanting to run to the children. "Just a minute," he told her. "Give them a chance to get out of the car and get their things."

Gina was now rounding the car to get to the other side and open a door there. A few moments later, she appeared in view again carrying a bouncy toddler on her arm. He turned his head this way and that and cried out in a high-pitched voice. Ewan smiled to himself. What a cute little guy. But probably fast as a dart once his feet hit the ground. He had seen such little kids before and knew how quickly they could run off if given half a chance. He'd better watch that one carefully so he didn't get into any trouble pulling things off of shelves or disappearing from sight.

Gina took a big shopping bag from the back

of the car and then checked whether all doors were closed. Her one daughter waited impatiently, pointing to the center, while the other still stood close to the car, as if she wanted to get back in it again and hide.

Gina gestured with the hand holding the large shopping bag for her to come along. He realized as he watched her how three children were literally a handful. With her boy in her arms and carrying the bag, she was unable to physically shepherd the girls to the center. But it seemed this shy little one did need that.

He leaned down and clipped the leash off Fuzzy. Then he opened the door for her. "Go to Gina," he said. "Go and say hello."

The dog shot away, running down the path past an elderly couple who were just coming up to the center. The woman smiled as she watched the dog breeze by and said something to her husband.

Fuzzy ran for the group moving up behind them. The reluctant girl in the red T-shirt caught sight of the dog and her eyes widened. Fuzzy ran to Gina and sniffed her legs, then turned to the shy little girl. She looked up at her as if she understood that this was the reason Ewan had sent her out. The girl sank to her knees and looked the dog over with an excited expression. Gina said something, probably telling her she could pet it. The girl reached out a tentative hand. Fuzzy sniffed her fingers and then licked her hand. The girl laughed.

Ewan felt a warmth spread through his chest. He had hoped for this response. For some lightness to break the tension when they arrived. The girl was obviously uncertain in new surroundings, and while Gina exuded calm, he bet she was nervous too, about meeting all of them and getting the okay to sell her products. It was inevitable to feel a little strain when doing something you had never done before.

He ambled down the path. Gina watched her daughter interact with the dog, then suddenly, as if feeling he drew near, she looked up. As their eyes met, Ewan's breath caught a moment. He had waited for this all week long. Anticipated this moment with the eagerness of a wildlife photographer creating the right circumstances to catch that rare bird in front of his lens. There she was. On his territory. With that gorgeous smile.

"Ewan!" Gina had no hand free to raise in greeting, but he saw how she started forward in his direction. "Thank you for asking us to come here. I love it already."

He answered her smile. "That's great. Good morning. Was it easy to find?"

"Oh yes, there are signs everywhere." She tilted her head a little. "And you had messaged me directions last night."

Ewan felt his cheeks heat up. "That probably wasn't necessary," he rushed to say. "But just to make sure, you know…" He felt like a blundering schoolboy, but Gina's eyes were warm.

"That was very thoughtful. After all, last time I came here I was as young as the girls, and my dad was driving." She waited a moment before adding, "Those were good times."

He noticed how her mouth tightened a little as she said it and he wondered if it hurt to think about those good times.

The girl with the yellow shirt pulled at his sleeve. "Sir? Are we going to see bears? It was you with the bear, right, in the photo? I want to see real bears. They are awesome."

"I'm afraid I can't promise you real bears today. But I can teach you a lot about wildlife. And there are mounted animals inside."

The girl seemed a little disappointed at the announcement, but the shy girl looked up and said, "Oh good. I never did like bears."

"But you do like dogs," Ewan said. "Her name is Fuzzy. What is yours?"

"Ann."

"I should have introduced the children," Gina said. "That is Stacey, and this here is little Barry." She held the boy out to him with obvious pride. He reached out a hand and tickled the child on the cheek. The boy studied him with a pensive look. For a moment Ewan wondered if he looked a lot like his daddy. That had been one lucky man to have a gorgeous family like this.

Then again, not so lucky as he had passed away at a young age. Ewan didn't know how exactly, but he hoped that perhaps he could sometime learn more about Gina's past. To understand her better. What she had been through, where her fears came from. How he might help her feel at home here.

"Well, Stacey and Ann," he said to the little girls, "how would you like to see inside the center?"

"I guess we have to," Stacey said with a sigh. "But I'd rather go look for bears."

"Ewan already said there aren't any here," Gina responded with an edge in her voice. "I bet there are lots of fun things to do *inside* the center, Stacey."

Stacey pulled a face at her and ran ahead to the door that the elderly couple had left open for them. Fuzzy followed her in a trot, barking. "Hey, wait for me," Ann yelled and followed them.

Gina smiled at him. "Thanks for involving Ann in it. She was a little uh…apprehensive because of Stacey's big stories about bears."

"I'm sorry if my photo caused the commotion. Most kids love the mounted animals. I was just trying to…"

"Don't worry," Gina said with a kind insistence in her voice. "I just happen to have twins who are complete opposites, character-wise. Stacey wants to try everything and isn't afraid of anything, while Ann jumps at her own shadow. I want you to know because we are going to spend the day together and…"

Ewan wasn't listening anymore after that. He was walking here with a beautiful woman by his side who smiled up at him and said they were going to spend the day together. What else did he need to know?

He mentally kicked himself and tuned back in to what she was saying. It was important to know things about the people he guided. This was a professional thing. He was on the job, he was showing them around as a guide at the center, he had to act like…he knew what he was doing?

He almost had to laugh. It was strange, but he had just never felt this way before.

GINA GLANCED AT EWAN. It had struck her before that he had kind eyes and that he could listen well, but now she had the impression he was so fully focused on her that he wasn't seeing anything else. It made her feel kind of…special. As if this invitation wasn't about finding a new job and having income after being fired, but…something more personal.

Barry cried out and Ewan said, "He dropped his toy." He leaned down to retrieve the soft cuddle blanket with zebra head that Barry adored. "There you go, little one." He reached it out and Barry grabbed at it, squealing.

Gina said, "He doesn't want to go anywhere without it. It has a clip so I can attach it to his clothes like you do with a pacifier on a chain, but somehow he manages to get it off every time." She reached for the clip, but Barry pulled the toy away from her grasp.

"Let me help you," Ewan said. He put his hand over the toy so Barry couldn't move it. Gina took hold of the clip. Her fingers brushed Ewan's hand a moment. "Don't hold it too tightly," she said. "I can't move it up to clip it to the neckline of his sweater."

Ewan released his grip a little. Barry used one hand to strike at Ewan's hand. "Let go," he cried in his most indignant tone. "My zebwa."

Ewan smiled at the cute way Barry pronounced the word. Gina suddenly didn't want this moment to end. She wished she could just stand here and feel the warm weight of her little boy against her and then this man standing beside her, almost like…they were a family?

No. She didn't have a complete family anymore. Her husband was gone.

She pulled away from Ewan and said quickly, "I have to go see where the girls are. Stacey can be very wild and…" Unable to continue without her voice becoming unsteady, she rushed to the center's open doors. Her heart beat fast as if she was escaping some dangerous situation. Why had she decided to come here? For the chance to sell her baking? Or also to see Ewan again?

What did he do to her?

She didn't want to think about it.

Not now. This was way too important to get wrong. She needed to convince the lady who ran the gift shop that her products were a worthy addition. She had been fired and she needed a new position. She had to focus. Get the job done.

Inside the light was dimmer, and she had to stop walking so fast to let her eyes adjust. To her left was a reception desk where the elderly couple who had come up ahead of them were asking for information about a walk they wanted to do. They had read about it in a hiking magazine. The friendly middle-aged woman behind the desk explained that it wasn't an easy walk because the terrain was rough, going up and down, and it was better to have some hiking experience and wear sturdy shoes. The woman of the couple laughed heartily and said, "Don't worry about that, we've hiked all around the world. We're both very experienced and come well prepared."

Gina wished she had their confidence. She should feel very experienced, both at parenting and running a business. She had been a mother for seven years now, and the pizzeria had blossomed with her doing various tasks: working as a hostess, doing marketing, running promotions, thinking up decorations and making changes to the menu. If it hadn't been for the debts, it would have continued to be a successful restaurant. She should be proud of what she had accomplished. She wasn't some college student who came in here looking for a summer job; she had things to offer them, most of all her enthusiasm and dedication to what she did. Could she rely on her gut feeling that this opportunity at the center was a chance she had to take?

"It can climb way up across the rocks," she heard Stacey's voice from somewhere to her right. "It's not at all like a goat on a petting farm."

Gina suppressed a grin at Stacey's know-all attitude. She followed the sound of the voice to where the girls stood side by side in front of a large glass panel. Reaching all the way up to the high ceiling, it encased a scene of mounted animals in their natural environment. Two mountain goats were jumping across rocks while a third one had a baby right by its side. Gina recalled this panorama had already been there when she had come here as a little girl with her father. He had shown her the animals, told her what they were and where they lived. She had been in awe of the presentation with the large glass wall separating her from the animals who were to her mind almost alive. Sometimes she could have sworn she saw an ear twitch. She had even had a dream once that they started moving and broke through the glass to get free.

Standing in the center again, looking at how

realistically the animals' postures had been recreated, she wished Dad was still alive to be here with her. That she could put his grandson in his arms. But he had never seen any of her children. He had been swept away from them by a sudden heart attack, there in his beloved orchard. She knew he had lived a full life and had been a very grateful man who had died in the place he cherished, on the ranch that had meant so much to him and his father and grandfather before that. But still it felt like such a shame he wasn't alive today to spend time with his grandchildren.

Stacey looked up at her. "Barry likes it, Mom, look at his face."

Gina turned her eyes away from the scene that held such bittersweet memories to focus on her little boy. He looked at the animals with fascination and extended a chubby hand. "Pet," he demanded. "Pet," he said again, like he did when she took him into the barn to see the donkeys and guinea pigs.

She had to laugh despite her melancholy. "No you can't pet those, Barry. They are wild animals. They live in the mountains where they roam free."

"Daddy loved the mountains," Stacey said. "I guess Barry takes after him."

Gina's stomach filled with ice at the idea that Barry would be anything like his father, loving mountains, snow, skiing, adventure. Danger. No, she would make sure he loved no such things. That he would stay far away from anything that could hurt him.

Then why did you bring him here? a voice inside questioned her. *Because you love baking? Or wanted to see Ewan again? What if your decision endangers your children?*

She turned away quickly. "Come along, Mommy has to show her baked goods to the lady in the gift shop."

"Can't we look around? There's so much to see here." Stacey gave her a pleading look. "That gift shop must be dull."

"Don't criticize. You haven't even seen it."

"But you will talk for hours. I want to see the center. And play outside." Stacey pulled at her leg. "Please, Mommy."

"I can show them around," Ewan's voice said from behind.

Gina swallowed hard. She had been impolite walking away like that. He had no idea, of course, how his kindness reminded her of other times in her life. Happy times that she missed and ached for.

Ewan appeared in her line of vision. He

didn't show any sign of feeling irritated at her behavior. On the contrary, he was smiling. "Why don't you go and talk to Granny, and I will show the girls around. They are right that there is so much to see here, all fun things."

Gina hesitated a moment. She knew that if she insisted and took the girls along, Stacey would be sulking, pulling faces, sighing and making half-loud comments, and she did want to make a good impression when she met her new boss. *Hopefully* her new boss…

"Okay," she said, and Stacey whooped. She asked Ewan, "Can we go and play outside?"

"No, we're going to look around inside. There are more animals here like those." He pointed at the glass wall. "And we can do a quiz."

Stacey looked doubtful.

"It's really fun," he promised, "and you can win prizes."

Now Stacey was all on fire. "I will get first prize," she announced and took Ann's arm. "Come on, let's go see the other animals."

They walked away. Ewan leaned over to Gina and said in a low voice, "When you meet Granny and introduce your products to her, don't make it sound like she needs help or anything. She is allergic to that idea. You act like you, uh…need the opportunity. I know it's not what you want maybe, but… Granny is really independent. Letting her feel like she can still do everything on her own is way better."

"I know people like that," Gina assured him. "I will do my best to, uh…" *Look needy?* "Reconcile all interests."

"I knew you would be diplomatic." He looked relieved as he touched her hand a moment. "We have some big anniversary celebrations coming up during the year and they mean a lot to Granny. It's great if we can all lend a hand to make it work out. Till later, then." He turned around and walked away, Fuzzy following him like a shadow.

Gina stood for a few seconds, still feeling the warmth of his hand. How good it was to talk and confide in each other, share a moment of understanding about having to help this elderly lady without her feeling like she was losing her independence. It could be their little project, something they did together.

Together. It was such a nice word. Like a warm blanket to sink into, or hot chocolate on a cold winter's day.

She sighed in satisfaction, then felt the weight of the shopping bag in her hand. She had her products to promote. It was up to her now. Ewan had opened a door for her, but she had to step through it on her own and make it work. Could she?

Time to find out!

EWAN WASN'T SURE he had handled it in the right way. He thought it was better for Gina to meet Granny one-on-one without him hovering by her side trying to smooth the way like some helicopter parent. Gina didn't need that. She was wonderful, her baked goods were great, and as soon as Granny saw that, she would be sold on the idea of letting Gina sell things here at the center. It was as easy as that.

But right now, as he followed the excited twins from item to item, he wondered if he shouldn't have gone with her. Maybe she felt like he had invited her here and had now abandoned her. He hadn't even introduced her to Granny.

He shook his head in irritation. There was no point to second-guessing. He had made the decision based on his gut feeling, and he had to believe it would turn out right. That was how he lived, and it worked for him.

"Look," Ann said. "Paw prints."

"Oh, yes this is a really fun thing. This box holds sand and those stamps over there are all molded to resemble the paws of animals. Pick one up and you can make prints in the sand."

Ann had already chosen one and tried. "Oh, look. I think it's a bird."

"Very good. What kind of bird?"

"A big one," Stacey said. "Look at the size of the prints."

"Right. Do you know any big birds that live in this area?"

Ann frowned hard. "Maybe crows?" she tried doubtfully.

"A bird of prey!" Stacey cried, then her expression set. "But I don't know any names."

"That's not a problem. There is a chart on the wall there with birds of this region. You go and have a look at them and then come back to me to tell me what you think this might be."

The girls immediately went to check out the chart. Ewan straightened up and rolled back his shoulders. He felt a tension he normally never had on a Saturday morning. He would be showing around families, chatting, laughing, having a good time. But a lot was hanging on this Saturday morning. Would Granny like Gina as much as he did? It seemed a given but what if he was wrong?

From the corner of his eye, he saw Stacey walk away from Ann, who was completely absorbed in the bird chart. Stacey peeked into the dark opening that led into their movie theater. It was a grand name for a small room with about twenty chairs where people could watch footage of nature documentaries that had been shot in the Rockies. Usually families with children skipped those presentations as kids found them boring, but senior citizens appreciated them and often sat watching for quite some time.

Stacey turned away from the door in a jerk. He saw a look on her face that made his heart skip a beat. Panic. It was at odds with her open and adventurous character. It fitted shy Ann, not her. What had she seen that had shocked her?

He walked over to her and leaned down to look her in the eye. "Is something wrong, Stacey?"

She bit her lip before she replied, "Ann can't go in there and look. She will start crying."

"Okay," he said at once, struck by the seriousness in her features. "We won't go in there." He had no idea why, but he knew, instinctively, that he had to listen to her.

"Stacey!" Ann waved at her sister. "I think I know what bird it is. Come and look."

Stacey said to him, "We won't go in there, right?"

"We won't, I promise."

"Good." Relief flooded her face. "Thanks." And she rushed to her sister.

Ewan looked at them a moment as they stood chatting and pointing out birds on the chart, then he stuck his head around the door of the movie theater and had a look at what was playing on the screen. A giant mass of snow rolled down a mountain, tearing along everything in its path. It had to be pretty frightening to a child. Wasn't it sweet of Stacey to take her sister's nature into account in that way?

He went to them and asked if they wanted to guess what bird it was. They then played with the paw prints some more, and also made prints of their hands in the sand. Stacey was boisterous again, and Ann also seemed to thaw and enjoy herself.

Ewan quickly guided them past the door leading to the offensive footage and continued the tour by taking them upstairs for more mounted animals and a giant jigsaw puzzle they had to complete by dragging the pieces into the right place. He noticed that Stacey was looking at the sunlit windows every few minutes, and he also wanted to go out there and enjoy the fine day. But Gina had to join them then. He couldn't wait to show her the garden. It was a little early in the season for blossoming plants, but he could show them the various games you could play there.

While Ann was putting the last jigsaw puzzle piece in place, Stacey touched his arm. She gestured for him to lean down all the way to her and whispered so he could barely hear it, "If there are avalanches in these mountains, can they get here?"

Her eyes were wide and questioning.

Ewan took his time to answer. He was sorry that the images of the documentary had shocked her, but he wasn't about to sweep her fear under the carpet or downplay the danger.

"Avalanches often occur high in the mountains where there is a lot of snow packed together. But once the snow starts moving, it can slide a long way down. So when this center was built here they also made fences on the mountainside, higher up. When the snow does come down, it hits those fences and they break the speed. Most of the time it stops the avalanche altogether."

"But not always?" Stacey asked with tilted head.

"It's already spring now so the snow is melting," he said truthfully. "That means the risk is getting smaller. You don't have to worry about it. As long as you don't go into the actual mountains, you are quite safe."

She nodded with a thoughtful expression. "Ann is very afraid of it. She even dreams about it."

"But you have never been here, right?" he asked, confused as to why a little girl would be so afraid of avalanches. "Did you live somewhere with lots of snow?"

"No, we lived in the city." Stacey glanced at Ann, who had completed the puzzle and was now at the computer where a reward was unlocked for her. "But Daddy often went skiing. He loved mountains and snow."

Ewan still didn't quite understand. Had Ann felt threatened by the snow because it had taken her Daddy away from her on trips? Things a child worried about in the daytime might translate into dreams in a twisted way, taking her to the snowy slopes she resented, maybe?

Ann called to Stacey to come and see the reward. Ewan followed and explained that they could print off the card that they were seeing on screen and take it home.

"The printer is in that corner." He pointed.

Ann pressed the enter button and ran to the printer at once. She seemed to have forgotten she hadn't wanted to come here. It was very good to see her so excited and happy.

Stacey said with a sigh, "It's too bad you have avalanches here. When Mom hears about that, she won't want to come here anymore. She won't let us come either." She looked up at him with worried eyes. "But I like it here. I want to come here more often. Can't you make sure she doesn't find out?"

He wanted to say that a grown-up like Gina would certainly know, but then reconsidered. Maybe Gina hadn't thought it through beyond her desire to sell her products and fill the financial hole left in her budget by her sudden dismissal. Maybe she would realize as she was here that this environment was foreign to her and represented things she didn't like.

How could he stop her from walking away? Could he even?

"Please?" Stacey pleaded, slipping her hand into his. "Ann likes it here too and usually she doesn't like places. She wants to stay at home most of the time."

"I'm sure we can think of ways to entice your mother to come here more often," he heard himself promise. For the little girl's sake, of course, but also for his own. He wanted to see much more of this intriguing little family.

CHAPTER SIX

GINA STOOD OPPOSITE the elderly lady Ewan had told her about, and doubts assailed her at once as to the viability of her mission. This woman, although white haired and of frail build, exuded a willpower that impressed her. This wasn't someone who would easily ask for help, or accept it.

"So you are Gina Williams," Granny said, studying her with a long look. "Ewan was so complimentary about your products. He seemed to think they shouldn't be missed by the many people who come here."

Gina flushed. Ewan hadn't actually tried any of her baked goods. He had obviously exaggerated to get her in. Still, she was here now and had to make her case. "I love baking. I was raised on a ranch with apple orchards, so even as children we learned to cook and bake with apples. I kept that up later. I used to bake once a month with my sister-in-law, Lily."

"Oh yes, I know she is married to your brother, Cade. I met the two of them once at a market where he was engraving wood. He is quite good at that."

Gina might have explained that Lily had also been her sister-in-law before she married Cade, because she was the sister of Gina's late husband, but it seemed like that would put a chill note into their conversation. She didn't want to go around in circles all of the time, ending up with the "I am a widow" line.

"Nowadays I do a lot of baking nights and on weekends. I've delivered buns and pies for town birthdays and anniversaries, even to the mayor. And…"

Granny raised a hand. "I don't need to hear a whole story. I just want to taste what you brought."

Right. Gina put down Barry and pulled the top see-through plastic container from her shopping bag. It was filled with glazed apple and cinnamon buns. She pulled the lid off and offered Granny a bun.

Barry cooed as he toddled away. She quickly picked him up and leaned him on her hip. He pulled a discontented face but didn't cry. Fortunately.

Granny chewed in silence. Gina tried to read

her expression, but it was blank. What if she didn't like it?

"Delicious," Granny said.

Gina breathed a sigh of relief. "I also have apple cake here. And apple pie." She reached into the bag but couldn't shift the heavy container with one hand.

"Could I hold that adorably little boy for you?" Granny asked.

"Oh, if you don't mind…"

"It's my pleasure." Granny reached out her arms, and Gina carefully transferred Barry to her. The little boy studied Granny's face a moment and then focused on the necklace she wore. His chubby hands grabbed at it.

"Careful!" Gina warned. "He is strong enough to rip it apart." She felt uncomfortable that her host was under attack, but Granny grinned. "It's a cheap necklace. I don't mind him exploring it at all. Gently now, little one." She guided his hand and he giggled.

Gina quickly unboxed the other items and offered Granny more treats. They both had to laugh when Barry tried to grab some too. "He must be hungry. I have something for him to nibble on."

"Could this help?" A giant man with a beard appeared beside them with a high chair. "I took it from the coffee corner," he explained. "That way the little troublemaker is cooped up a bit and you have your hands free."

"He is no troublemaker," Granny protested. "But he is a handful, I admit. Thank you, Grizzly." She explained to Gina, "This is Garrett, but we all call him Grizzly."

"Nice to meet you." Gina shook his hand.

Grizzly eyed the treats. "Can I also have a say in the selection process?"

Granny frowned at him. "I see. You only came over with the high chair so you could move in on the treats. You better keep them away from him, Gina, because he also has a bear's appetite."

"I only wanted to have a little try," Grizzly said with an exaggerated sad expression that made Gina laugh. She handed him an apple cinnamon bun. "Thank you for your excellent suggestion with the high chair. When I come here more often, I have to bring Barry's playpen."

She fell silent and flushed. The fiery feeling spread across her cheeks and neck. Why had she been so forward? "I'm sorry," she tried to backpedal. "You haven't even decided yet if you want my products and here I am, inviting myself in."

"Honey, there was never any doubt in my mind that I would add your baked goods to my offer. Ewan has excellent taste, so if he recommends you, it's a done deal. And now that I have tasted this, I'm even more convinced it's a wonderful idea."

"Yeah…" Grizzly mumbled around half the apple cinnamon bun he had pushed into his mouth.

"Don't talk with your mouth full," Granny berated him. "There is a small child here now and we all have to set a good example. I wouldn't want him to adopt your eating habits." She turned to Barry and tickled him under his chin. "It will be wonderful to hear a small voice around the building." She looked up at Gina and said, "I do hope you want to come and work here with us. It will mean a lot of extra exertion. After all, you only had to drive ten minutes to get to your old job. We are much further away."

"Just half an hour," Gina said. "That's definitely doable."

Granny kept looking concerned. "And all the baking you will have to do… It will take a lot of time and effort. It's all handwork and…"

"Oh, but I love to do it."

"And once you are here, you might need to

chip in with a little something here and there.
Once it's busier… We are also celebrating the
center's seventy-fifth anniversary this year so
there will be lots of extra activities."

"A big kickoff barbecue in a few weeks,"
Grizzly offered with a delighted grin.

Granny continued, "You will probably be
asked to help with ideas for activities or to lend
a hand getting things set up. I don't know if
you've realized…"

"I don't mind at all," Gina rushed to reassure her. Ewan had already mentioned the anniversary as something that would involve a
lot of extra work. It had seemed he thought she
could help with it to give Granny some much-
needed support. Seeing the kind elderly lady
in action, Gina was easily convinced to help
her. Imagine Granny working here for so many
years, investing her warmth and energy in the
center. Celebrating its anniversary had to be
a momentous occasion for her. She rushed to
say, "On the ranch there are so many chores
to do all day long. It's only natural for me to
lend a hand. I like to stay busy."

There was a moment's silence, and Gina had
a feeling that Granny's eyes saw right through
her and that the elderly woman understood that
she was often lonely and heartbroken. But then

Grizzly wiped his mouth with the back of his hand and said, "That's all decided, then. Welcome to our family."

He brushed Barry's head and walked off.

Granny sighed. "Can I never make a single decision myself?" But her eyes twinkled, and it didn't seem she was genuinely irritated. "You are hired, young lady. Along with your adorable assistant." She patted Barry's chubby hand, which immediately grabbed for her fingers. "I was told you also have two girls?"

"They're with Ewan."

"Oh yes, Ewan." Granny's eyes sparkled even more.

Gina quickly said, "He's showing them around. He knows so much about this place and the region."

"Yes, it's great when you can do a job you love." Granny clapped her hands together. "Coffee, then? I could use a cup and so could you I suppose."

CHAPTER SEVEN

WHEN EWAN AND the girls entered the gift shop area, they found Granny and Gina busy with a display of mugs with animal tails for handles. Gina was just moving one to a lower place and said with a sigh of satisfaction, "There, that is perfect."

"You really have an eye for it," Granny said. "I like it much better now."

"Granny," Ewan faked the reproach in his voice, "you can't put Gina to work like that. She's a guest here."

"Oh no. She works here. I hired her and she started right away. Ewan McAllister, meet your new colleague, Gina Williams."

"Pleased to meet you," Ewan said reaching out his hand.

Gina had obviously not expected him to complete the supposed introduction ritual, but after a moment's hesitation, she put her hand in his. He squeezed softly and smiled at her. "Wel-

come. I see that you quickly convinced everyone."

"Well, that cute little boy also helped,"
Granny said nodding at Barry, who was sitting
in a high chair, playing with his cuddly toy. "He
is so sweet and quiet. Barely makes a peep."

"Not like those two," Ewan said searching
for the girls, who were admiring all on offer.
"They talked a lot."

"I hope they weren't a bother," Gina said with
a probing look.

"Of course not. It's great that they are so cu-
rious. But my throat is parched from talking
so much."

"That's your cue, Gina," Granny said. "Fetch
the man some coffee."

Gina turned away with a smile. As soon as
she was out of earshot, Granny said in a whis-
per, "She is even more special than I gathered
when you suggested she come to work here.
I knew she had to be something else because
she had you interested but…"

"Hush." Ewan flushed again. This was starting to get annoying. "I only want to help her
find a job. Not… It's embarrassing to…"

"Yes, yes, I will shut up about it." Granny
made a reassuring gesture. "I just want you
to know how glad I am you brought it up. Her

sweets are delicious, and I think her personality fits right in here."

"Yes, we just have to make sure she doesn't find out about the avalanches," Ewan muttered. He was still not sure whether it had been a child's exaggerated impression of reality, or a serious issue.

"What?" Granny asked, but Gina was already returning with a mug of coffee for him. He accepted it with a grateful smile. "Just what I need."

"I don't know if you take any milk or sugar in it…" She looked ready to rush back and fetch what he wanted.

"No, no, I take it black. Thanks."

"Mom! Can we have this?" Stacey's voice resounded from the back of the gift shop area.

"Excuse me while I go see what they are *not* going to get." Gina wriggled her brows at him and disappeared.

Granny said, "She is such a positive, upbeat person. And I simply love her kids. She will fit right into our group." She squeezed his arm. "Thanks, Ewan, for bringing them here."

Ewan felt almost guilty that Granny was so excited while he had told Gina she needed a lot of help and… He also had an ulterior motive. He realized now that he had not brought

Gina here for Granny, or to provide delicious baked goods to the center's guests, but to see more of her.

He hastily focused on sipping his coffee. It was too hot still and he burned his tongue. That happened when you weren't paying attention. He should know better. Losing focus was dangerous. He had to be nice to her and help her adjust here, but he had to keep any other thoughts in check. She was probably not looking for romance.

That makes two of us, he addressed himself sternly. Returning to civilization had been hard. It had proved to him how much of a loner he was and how much he needed to be able to do his own thing. Living in remote places, he had never had much of a chance for casual dating. During his training, he had met other nature enthusiasts and had also watched some team up and continue their work in nature conservation together. He had thought back then that if he ever fell in love, it had to be with someone who shared his passion for nature and adventure. That if he ever got together with someone, they'd be like Mom and Dad were, traveling the world together. A widow with three young children wasn't likely to follow him to Asia to study snow leopards.

Besides, if they became involved, he would become an instant father figure, and he felt completely unfit to be anything like that. Sure, he could entertain kids when they came to the center, teaching them to make a birdhouse or taking them into the woods on the adventure trail. But raising children required a completely different skill set. He had zero experience with it and doubted that his character lent itself to fatherhood. He imagined that, especially with little girls, parenting had to be done with great tenderness and tact, while he was very practical and straightforward. So it was great to be friends with Gina and help her settle at the center, but he should definitely not be entertaining any other thoughts.

"It isn't much of a garden," Stacey said with a critical look around. "There aren't any flowers. Just a lot of small plants."

Gina opened her mouth to explain to her daughter, but Ewan beat her to it.

"In spring the plants still have a lot of growing to do," he said. "When summer comes around, you will see how beautiful it looks."

"Can we come back here in summer, Mommy?" Ann asked, squeezing her hand.

Ewan looked at Gina and said with a grin, "I hope you will be back here before that."

Gina felt her cheeks heat up. "I think we will be coming here more often, girls. Mommy is going to work here."

Stacey tilted her head. "Why? You work at the Western store in town. If you have two jobs, you will have even less time for us."

Now Gina's face was truly on fire. It felt like Ewan would realize what a bad mother she was, leaving her children while she went to work. But she only did it because she needed money to pay the bills.

Ewan said, "It's a sad thing that grown-ups have to spend so much time working. But it's better when you can do it in a nice environment. I work here, and every day I feel grateful I can do this job." He gestured around him. "Isn't it pretty? The forest, the mountains."

Mountains… Gina realized she had consciously kept her gaze away from them until now. She didn't want to see them, admire them. People thought they were pretty with the snow on top, but she knew better. They weren't beautiful, they were dangerous. They had stolen Barry away from her.

She held on tighter to his little namesake in her arms.

As if he sensed it, little Barry wrestled to be released. "Walk," he demanded. "Walk!"

Knowing he would get louder if he didn't get his way, Gina lowered him to the ground and let him walk ahead of her, holding him by his hands. He giggled happily.

A few paces away, Ewan was explaining something to the girls. Usually Stacey didn't like much talking, preferring to run around and play, but now she listened with interest.

Gina smiled to herself. Ewan seemed to have a very special influence on everyone. He was different from any man she had ever met. And he had a way with children that amazed her. Maybe he had grown up in a large family and had always cared for his younger brothers and sisters.

How do you even know he doesn't have any children of his own? a small voice in the back of her head asked. *You know next to nothing about him. Only that he doesn't wear a wedding ring.*

She bit her lip a moment realizing she had looked at his hands to make sure. Why?

"Mom!" Stacey waved at her. "Look! There are plants here that you can smell. Just rub the leaves and try to make out what it is."

Gina came over as quickly as Barry's toddling allowed. She let go of him a moment to reach down and rub a leaf. She lifted her fingers to her nose and inhaled. "It's like lemon."

"Right. And this one is like…" Stacey pointed excitedly at the next one.

Gina leaned down to try. She widened her eyes as the scent invaded her nostrils. "Licorice."

"Right. Ewan just told us the plants are here for people to try and guess their scents. I never knew leaves had scents. Only flowers."

"This garden was specially designed," Ewan said, "to let people use all of their senses. Not just sight but also smell and touch."

Ann looked around her. "What do we have to touch?" she asked curiously.

Ewan gestured ahead. "The big sign over there. Go and have a look."

The girls ran over right away. Gina reached out again to rub the plant with the lemon scent. It was so fresh and invigorating. She wanted that in her own garden.

Suddenly she became aware that Barry wasn't clinging to her leg anymore. She turned her head quickly to see him toddle down the dirt path after the girls. There was nothing particularly threatening about his situation, but her heart raced, and a stab of guilt pierced her chest. She should keep an eye on him always. He was still so little. He could get hurt.

Ewan was with the little boy in a quick movement. Gina expected that he would scoop him up, but Ewan just stayed beside him watching him as he walked on unsteady feet, holding his arms out to stay balanced. The path was uneven, and little Barry had to do his very best not to fall.

Suddenly he stumbled. Gina gasped, and her hands flew forward in a reflex to catch her sweet little baby even though she was too far away.

Barry's little hands had also reached out instinctively to break his fall, and he lay there a moment half propped up on his arms. The air seemed to be so silent, waiting for him to break into a wail.

Ewan didn't reach out to touch him, he didn't even say a word. He just watched.

Barry took a deep breath, then put his hands on the path to push himself up again. He threatened to tip to the right, and Ewan's strong suntanned hand was there in a flash to steady him. But he let him do most of the work by himself. Barry stood again, grinning ear to ear. Then he toddled on toward his sisters.

Gina reached Ewan and said, "What did you do that for?"

Ewan looked at her, with a puzzled expression. "Sorry?"

"You were close enough to stop him from falling. You could have caught him before he hit the ground."

"It's a dirt path. Besides, little children often fall, and they usually don't hurt themselves. You saw how he responded. He got right back onto his feet."

Gina blinked. "Most of the time he cries when he falls over."

"But this time he didn't." Ewan smiled at her. "He is too excited about being out here. He wants to explore. And that will help him get steadier on his feet."

Gina frowned hard. "So I should just let him fall because then he learns something?"

Ewan held her gaze. "You make it sound almost like a crime."

"Well, I love my children, and I don't want them to get hurt." Gina brushed by him to go to the girls. Barry was clinging to Ann's leg now. Stacey ran her fingers over the big wooden plaque. It was full of dots.

"I don't know what this is," she said to Gina. "Is it some secret message? Or code?"

"Maybe it's Morse code," Ann suggested.

"No," Ewan's voice said from behind. "It's braille. Those are letters you can feel with your fingertips."

"That seems difficult." Stacey gave him a pensive look. "Why would anyone think of a language that is so difficult?"

"Well, when you had to learn how to read, did you find that easy?"

"I did," Ann said seriously, and Gina saw the amusement twitch around Ewan's lips.

Stacey gave her sister a sideways glance. "You are weird."

"Stacey, I don't want you to say that to your sister. You are just different, that's all."

"That's right," Ewan said. "People are different, and so languages have to be different too. Now, when you learned how to read, the teacher taught you the letters…" He picked up a stick and drew an A in the sand. "You knew this was A. And then you could make words like *and* or *apple*. In braille, this is *A*." He pointed out a single dot on the plaque. "So just like when you see this drawing and call it *A*, someone else feels this dot and calls it *A*. It's the same thing."

"Oh," Stacey said with a frown. "But I think

A and *C* look very different. These look like all the same dots to me."

"Well, when you look closely at letters, they all consist of lines." Ewan drew the *A* again. "See? A line running down to the left, then one to the right and a line to connect them in the middle. In the same way, braille consists of dots. Once you understand how each combination of dots has meaning, it's just as easy as reading letters."

"I think it's really special," Ann said, "and I'd like to learn a few letters."

Ewan nodded. "Okay. I can teach you a word."

While he was pointing out things to her on the plaque, Gina looked at his excited expression. He was totally in the moment teaching this little girl about braille like he did so every day. Maybe he did, working here. Still his kind attention felt…special? Like it was meant just for them.

Barry cooed and she picked him up. He rested his head on her shoulder. His little hands were dirty with sand, and she cleaned them automatically. Suddenly she turned her head. "Where is Stacey?"

A new jolt of worry shot through her. With three children you had to pay attention at all times. But having lived on the ranch for so long now, she had gotten used to others being there to take care of the children alongside her. Mom, Cade, Lily. There was always someone to watch the girls and keep them in check. Today she was out on her own and…making a mess of it.

"Stacey!" she cried out.

EWAN LOOKED UP. He straightened at once as he saw the look on Gina's face. She was pale, and her eyes looked panicked. He said quickly, "She can't have gone far. I'll go and find her."

He rushed down the dirt path. Just around the bend he saw Stacey sitting on her haunches pricking into the dirt with a stick. She looked dejected. Ewan stopped in his tracks. He had expected the girl to have run off to do something wild and exciting, and now this…

He wasn't sure how to respond. Gina had obviously not liked the way he had handled the situation with little Barry. He should have caught him; he should have protected him, guarded him against the unpleasant experience of falling. What would Gina want him to do now?

He realized he had no idea, and maybe it didn't even matter. Because he couldn't live his life doing what other people thought he should do. He should do what he himself thought was right.

He went over to her and sat on his haunches to get to eye level with her. "Hey. Did you hear that bird call just now? Do you know what it is?"

Stacey shook her head. "Ann is always so smart," she said in a low tone. "She liked learning to read and write, didn't think it was hard at all. Mom and Grandma were telling her all the time how wonderful that was. They admired her. They don't admire me."

Ewan studied her with a pang of sadness inside. He knew what it was like to feel less capable than others. He had never been much of a book person. He had learned a lot by doing, by being out in the wilderness. He hadn't been a straight-A student. He had gotten his degree with decent grades, but only because he had studied hard. Because he had wanted to show his teachers and potential employers, who would look at his results, that he wanted this degree. But it had been a constant struggle. He could understand what this little girl was feeling right now.

"You know how I just said people are all different? You and Ann look a lot like each other on the outside, because you are twins, but you are very different on the inside."

"I know that. Ann is nice and quiet and sweet, and I am wild and irresponsible." Stacey hung her head even more. "It's not that I want to be, most of the time. I just see something I want to have a close look at, and then I run over without thinking. It's not like I want to make Mom worried. Not really."

"I understand. When I was your age, I also liked to explore. I wandered off and my parents were very worried. But they never told me that I couldn't do things. They helped me to learn the skills to take care of myself in an outdoor environment. They made me understand what was safe and what wasn't. If you want to, I can teach you."

Stacey looked up at him, hope in her eyes. "Really?"

"Yes. In fact, I think it's very important since you're going to be spending more time here now that your mother is going to work with us." Excitement rushed through him as he spoke those words. Gina was actually going to work with them. She was going to be part of their team, part of their lives. That was a great prospect. "I can teach you and Ann a lot of little tricks that are vital when you are outside a lot. How to tell what weather is coming by looking at the skies. How you can find your way back when you are lost. How to use certain tools."

Stacey's expression was wide open with joy at the idea. "I'd love to learn that. That is useful, not stuff from books that I keep forgetting." Then the light in her eyes dimmed. "Mom probably won't let us learn that. She doesn't want us to try anything. She thinks everything is dangerous."

She hung her head again and ran her finger across the holes she had pricked in the dirt with her stick. "Ever since Daddy died…"

Ewan swallowed hard. He'd had no idea how much the loss of their father had impacted these children, this little family. How afraid Gina was of anything happening to her little ones after she had already lost her husband.

His heart ached for this little girl who looked so sad, but at the same time another feeling unfolded in his chest—determination to make it better. Somehow.

"There you are!" Gina came running toward them, holding Barry in her arms. "Stacey, you can't just run off without saying where you're going. I was really worried."

Stacey shot to her feet and forced a smile. "I heard a bird I wanted to find in the treetops. I know I shouldn't have run off. I'm sorry."

Gina's expression softened. "Well, it is an exciting place, and I can understand you want to know more. But you have to stay with us. We are all going to learn about it together, okay?"

"Okay." Stacey nodded and started to skip ahead of them farther down the path. She hadn't said a word about being sad or feeling less loved than her sister because of her trouble learning. Ewan frowned as he studied her narrow back. That was a little girl who hid her sadness from her mother. Maybe because it was difficult to tell the people you loved the truth.

Or because she realized her mother had a hard life and she didn't want to make it any harder on her?

Either way it was sad.

"You look pensive," Gina said softly.

He jerked to attention. With groups he was guiding, people expected him to give them a good time and weren't interested in how he felt. Her perceptiveness was something new entirely. He almost felt uncomfortable and ready to deny he had anything particular on his mind.

"I was just thinking—" he quickly considered his options "—that if the children are going to come here more often, with you, they should learn a few basic survival skills."

"Survival?" Gina echoed, her eyes wide. "They aren't going to be in any danger, right? It is safe here? You said there were no bears."

"There aren't. But children benefit from knowing more about their environment. How to navigate with a compass, or how to tell the weather is changing by listening to the birds and animals in the forest."

"They aren't going to be out and about by themselves. If they come here, it will be with me and under my supervision." Gina sounded stern.

"I see," Ewan said before asking innocently, "And do you know how to navigate with a compass or tell the weather is changing by…"

"I don't have to." She didn't even let him finish. "I won't be out and about in bad weather. I'm a sunny-skies outdoor person. I only do things that are safe."

Ewan gave her a sideways glance. "But the weather can change quickly close to mountains. You can't predict that."

"We won't be going into the mountains. We can take a walk around this garden, fine, but nothing more. That's not what we're here for."

Ewan nodded, even though he hardly agreed. He had to think about this better. Find a way to teach the girls some skills. Even if they never needed them here, it would be an asset for the rest of their lives. But he had to go about it carefully. Maybe involve Granny. Have her talk to Gina.

Or Grizzly? Someone other than him. He had made her upset by letting little Barry fall.

See how you don't know anything about raising children? a voice inside taunted him. *She barely agreed to work here, and you're already turning her against you. If you had only caught Barry in your arms, she would have smiled at you and appreciated your help.*

But it hadn't seemed necessary. Even now he didn't see why his behavior had been wrong. The child seemed to be happy enough bouncing on his mother's arm.

Still, Gina had been upset, and she was the little boy's mother. She probably knew best.

Ewan reached out and ran his finger across Barry's chubby hand. "Is he okay now? I'm sorry if you had really expected me to catch him, but I didn't think it could do any harm. I guess he falls over at home as well. It's all part of learning how to walk properly."

"It's different for you since he isn't your child." Gina cuddled Barry with a sweet smile. "As his mother I just can't bear to see him cry." Suddenly she focused on him with her beautiful eyes. But they weren't smiling at him; they were rather guarded. "I'm grateful you gave me the chance to come here and get a job. But... Please leave raising my children to me. You don't understand how it is."

He hadn't expected her to say it out loud and it hurt. It wasn't like he had messed up on purpose. "I never meant to..." he began, but Gina cut across him.

"People seem to think they can always interfere with my life because I'm a widow and don't have a man by my side. But I'm working very hard to rebuild my life, our life as a family, and I don't need everyone's opinion about how I should do it."

"That's understandable," he said meekly. He could explain that he had only wanted little Barry to develop a bit of independence and that his choice to do things differently was no criticism of her parenting skills. But he didn't want to anger her further and ruin the day for the kids. Stacey had found a bird's feather and was showing it off to Ann. They were both laughing. He wanted those little girls to have a wonderful Saturday at their center. He could address Gina's concerns later. For now, they had to soak up the sunshine and bask in the wonders of the wilderness.

CHAPTER EIGHT

"AND WE HEARD a cell phone when we were walking, but it was a bird," Stacey told her grandmother, gesturing wildly. "The bird can imitate all kinds of human sounds. Anything he hears in the woods and near the center. We didn't see him though. He was well hidden in the leaves."

Gina said, "I think you'd better go change now, Stacey. We're about to have dinner." She felt a bit guilty she had stayed away so long and all the Saturday chores had landed on Mom and Lily. Including preparing the big family dinner they always had on Saturday night. Mom made her famous vegetable soup, then there was steak and corn on the cob. The dessert was usually Gina's department—cake and ice cream. Lily had taken care of dessert this time, Mom had said. She wasn't allowed to look in the fridge.

Lily came back in, having gone to call Cade

for dinner. He was right behind her, and they were both laughing. Seeing their happy faces, Gina felt a tug inside, aching to have that kind of happiness again.

Today she had walked in the garden near the center with her children and a man by her side, almost as if they were a family. She had felt relaxed, at ease. She couldn't remember when she had last spent such a fun afternoon out. But Ewan wasn't her husband. She didn't have what others had. She was alone.

Cade looked at her. A slight frown formed on his brow. "Hey, sis. Had a good day? You look tired."

"It was a long day including the drive and all. But worth it. The kids had so much fun. Barry was asleep when we got here so I put him to bed right away. He had enough to eat at the center. Granny is a wonderful woman. I mean, Mrs. Grant, but everyone calls her Granny. She runs the gift shop. I can sell my baked goods there."

Cade didn't seem to be truly listening, though he did nod. As he turned to the tap to wash his hands, he said, "Look, I ran into Burt Bayliss this morning. He might need a waitress for his diner. I know it isn't ideal because it will mean you'll be away evenings, but Lily can put the kids to bed and…"

"Cade," Lily said, prodding him with her elbow, "let Gina decide for herself what she wants to do."

"Well, I never said she had to go out and work in the first place. She can live here for free if she wants to. She wanted to earn her own keep, and now that Travers turned her out…"

Gina cringed. "I only thought it was best to earn some money."

"Of course it is," Lily said, looking at her with a reassuring smile. "Cade should stop meddling. How did it go at the center? Did they like your products? If they tasted them, they must have agreed they are wonderful."

Cade said, "Gina just mentioned it was a long drive. She probably doesn't want to go out there frequently. A job closer to home is much better." He vigorously rubbed his hands dry. "You think about it and then call Bayliss. I'll write down his number for you."

"Cade…" Lily shook her head. "Let it be, for tonight, will you?" She winked at Gina. "Are the girls ready for dinner? I bet they will love the dessert."

"I'll go and see where they are," Gina offered, but her mother was just walking into the kitchen with a girl on each hand. "We are all ready to sit down and eat."

They gathered round the table. As Gina looked past their faces, she realized she would miss this once she had her own home again. But she needed a home of her own. A bit of independence. A way to decide things for herself, and not wonder if Cade agreed with her choices. He was a great big brother, but he was overprotective.

Just like you are with the kids? a small voice questioned her. *If you don't let Barry walk and explore on his own, he will never learn things. He didn't seem upset after the fall. Didn't Ewan have a point with what he said?*

Ewan isn't family, she argued back. *He doesn't have a right to tell me anything.*

"Do you want to say grace?" Mom asked Stacey. The little girl nodded, and they all joined hands. "Thank you, God, for the wonderful day we had at the center. Thank you for Ewan, he is really nice. Bless this food and help us be good. Amen."

"Amen," Mom said with a smile, but Cade had a huge frown now.

"Who is this Ewan?" Cade asked.

She flushed and felt like she was in high

school again and Cade had seen her talking to a classmate and immediately wanted to know who it was and what they had been up to.

"He knows everything about animals," Stacey said with a gesture.

"And about braille," Ann supplied. "He taught me how to read braille letters from a plaque. They are just like other letters but different."

Mom nodded appreciatively. "That sounds great."

Cade said, "Does he work at the center? What does he do there?"

"He shows people around, takes them out wildlife spotting. That sort of thing," Gina said.

"Hmm. College student?" Cade held out his bowl to Mom to fill with soup but kept looking at Gina.

"No," she said, suddenly feeling defensive, "he is more my age I guess."

"Oh."

Cade seemed to want to ask more, but Lily quickly passed him the plate with bread and said to Stacey, "Did they have mounted animals at the center?"

"Yes, a very big bear. And goats…sort of. They looked like goats."

"They were mountain goats," Ann said with her nose in the air.

"They still look like any goat," Stacey insisted.

The conversation went on about the sights and the garden. "There were also wooden animals there that Mr. Grizzly made. He's a wood artist," Ann explained. "He carves animals from logs. When you close your eyes, you can feel them with your hands and guess what they are."

"The garden has been designed to offer something for everyone," Gina said. "A very well-thought-out concept."

She barely tasted Mom's delicious soup as she waited for Cade to get back to the topic of Ewan McAllister. She knew her brother well enough to be certain he wasn't letting go. He wanted to know more. But she wasn't sixteen anymore. She owed him no explanation about any man she met. If she really wanted to regain some independence, she had to make that clear to Cade. That she appreciated his care for her, but that it was really time to find her own feet again.

The main course was served, and they chatted about the times Mom and Dad had taken them to the center and how much fun they had

had there. Gina wished Dad was still here to join in the conversation. At moments like these she always missed him even more than usual.

She was glad the others were talking so much that nobody noticed she was a little quiet.

Lily rose to go to the fridge and get out the special dessert she had made. "It's Italian," she said, and Cade's eyes lit.

"Tiramisu?"

"That's right. Homemade. I hope it had enough time to absorb all the flavors."

"I'm sure it did." Cade sat ready, his dessert bowl held out. "I want to try."

Gina had to smile. He was just like an eager puppy sometimes. Her irritation about his meddling faded, and she watched him with a warm smile as dessert was passed round and they tried a first bite. Mmms and aahs resounded. Lily beamed. Gina leaned back with the feeling that it wasn't bad she had been away for the day. Everyone had enjoyed what they did. Maybe she didn't have to be here all of the time. Maybe it was okay to stretch her wings and fly. Not far away—she would be back every day—but just…to experience new sights, new sounds, new people. It would bring a welcome distraction to her life. A fresh impulse.

After dinner the girls asked Lily to read them a story, and Cade said he'd do the dishes. "With you, Gina, so Mom can sit and enjoy her book."

Gina nodded her assent, even though she knew what Cade was up to. He wanted to use the time together to question her further. She mentally prepared herself to fend off his questions and defend her decision to start working at the center. After all, she had told Granny she would, and she could hardly go back on her word.

Cade submerged the first plates in the hot foaming water. He stared out of the kitchen window a moment into the dark yard. It seemed he was thinking about a way to open the conversation.

As the silence lingered, only broken by the sounds of the water splattering and the clean china being stacked on the table, Gina became uncomfortable. When Cade was interfering in a loud way, it was easy to claw back at him and not feel bad about it. But now he seemed so deep in thought and almost…emotional?

She didn't quite know how to handle her brother in that moment. She guessed he also had a lot of feelings about the situation: Barry's death and the way in which she had come home.

Cade wasn't the type to voice that though. He always plowed on, kept going, provided solutions to everyone's problems. Like Dad, he was a doer, not a talker. Maybe that was why they sometimes didn't see eye to eye.

Finally Cade said, "It was odd not having you around today."

That was about as good as an "I missed you." He'd never say that out loud; that wasn't his way. She tried to adopt a light tone. "You'll have to get used to it. Weekends are the busiest days at the center."

"Is it really necessary to go and work there?" He looked at her, his eyes probing. "Why do you feel the need to earn your own money?"

He had never asked it in such an outright manner. She didn't want to fob him off with a casual reply. She took her time to choose her words with care and still be clear. Speak her mind. "Because I can't live here for free forever. It was okay at the start when I was still pregnant and I had so much on my mind. But... Barry died two years ago. I have to get my life back on track." It sounded so simple, while it was so hard. But it was the only way to move forward. Having been at the center today, seeing how people liked her baked goods, welcomed her as a valuable addition, had boosted her self-confidence. She hadn't felt so good in a long, long time.

Cade twirled the dishcloth in the water. "I guess I, uh…feel a little apprehensive that you will want to move out. I've become quite attached to the girls and that little boy."

Her throat constricted. It wasn't like Cade to describe what he felt. The vulnerability in his features made her want to wrap her arms around him for a hug. But the issue he touched upon wasn't going to go away. She wanted to leave them. To go away from this safe haven and figure out life on her own. "I'm not gone overnight," she said softly.

"But you do want to leave." Cade looked her in the eye, and Gina saw no reason to lie. A few weeks back she might have reassured him quickly to avoid this discussion. To prevent him from asking questions and raising doubts she wasn't ready for. But today she felt stronger. Determined to stand her ground. She nodded slowly. "In due time, yes."

"Gina, we lost you once when Barry dragged you to the city and…we barely saw you, never got a chance to spend time with the twins. Don't do that again. Stay around here and… If you want to have your own house, okay, I can help you with that, even pay for it, if you want to."

"No, Cade. I don't want you to pay for it. I want to pay for it myself." Gina put her hand on his arm. Instead of anger she felt mostly sadness that he didn't see how this was for her. That he thought he was doing what was best for her family while she didn't agree. "Try and understand. I've had to depend on others for so long. I need to…"

"We are your family."

"I know. And I love you all very, very much. But… It's not good to stick around too long. You and Lily also need to have a life together. To build this ranch together. It's your ranch, not mine."

"We can cut you in." Cade looked eager. "If that is what…"

"No, Cade." She looked for the right words to get the message across. He simply didn't understand. She needed to explain it to him, without hurting his feelings. "I never wanted a ranch. I want a home for my family…and I also need to feel like I can make it on my own. That I am capable."

"You are. You know that." He rested both his hands on her shoulders. "You don't have to move away from here to prove a point."

Was she just trying to prove a point? Or was it more than that? "While working for Bud Travers, I realized all the time it was his business, not mine. I saw opportunities for the window display or the merchandise we stocked, but it wasn't for me to decide about those things. Now, with baking my own products for the center and being there in person to see people enjoy them, I can regain some of the creative joy I found when Barry and I had the pizzeria. You understand that?"

Cade took a deep breath. "Maybe. I think you bake great apple pie. But it's a hobby. Not a day job." He wasn't even giving her a chance to figure it out for herself. That was probably the worst part of it. Not whether she could actually live off her baking or not. She didn't claim to know that for sure. But that he didn't give her space to explore. He had drawn his conclusion before she had even started. That it would never work.

She shook off his hands. "I don't need you to tell me how to live, Cade. I can make my own decisions. And if they are wrong, then let them be. But at least I will be living the life I want for me and my family. Not someone else's plan." She walked out of the kitchen, almost bumping into Lily, who came back from reading to the girls.

"Gina…what…" Lily asked with a bewildered look, but Gina pushed past her. She was sorry that her beautiful day had ended on this low note. But the feelings she had experienced at the center also gave her strength. She was no longer floating like a boat without a paddle on an open sea, tossing and turning wherever the waves took her. She was steering now, directing the boat on a course she determined. She was going to make a good life for herself and her children. And no one was going to deflect her.

LILY STOOD, torn about whether she should go after her sister-in-law or leave her be. It had been a long day so maybe she was just worn out.

She turned to Cade, who stood at the sink. The frustration in his features told her the whole story. She suppressed a sigh. "Don't tell me you started about Bayliss again. A waitressing job isn't right for Gina."

"No, working at a center near mountains isn't right. You know how she hates mountains. What does she want there? Suddenly it's about needing creativity and never having been happy in the job with Bud Travers either. Because it was his business and not hers. I just don't get it."

"Maybe you don't have to. Let her make her own choices." Lily walked over. Her heart went out to her husband. He had a lot on his plate, and he felt too responsible for everything. But by taking this attitude he was losing the people he loved. "When Gina shares things with you, you don't have to respond right away with good advice. You have to think about your relationship first. About what your well-meant interference is doing to your bond. She probably feels like you don't value her opinion."

"I do. It's just that…" Cade swirled the cloth around in the dish water. "I can't get the image out of my head of Gina coming back here with two crying little girls, a few suitcases and nothing else to her name than the clothes on her back. I never want her to feel so vulnerable and alone again."

"I understand, Cade." Lily put her hand against his cheek. His skin was warm under her fingertips, reconnecting her with the man she knew and loved, with all his flaws. "I know how hard it was. I've been there."

They looked at each other a few moments, just saying nothing. Then Lily continued, "You provided a home for her and did everything to make her and the girls and little Barry feel safe. That's wonderful. But you can't make her happy. She has to find her own happiness again. In baking, in new friends. Maybe…in a new love?"

Cade held her gaze. "I don't want her to leave, Lily. I want to keep her here, where I can see her. Where I can protect her. Where I can make sure that nothing goes wrong again. This guy at the center… What is his name?"

Lily smiled softly. "You do know. Ewan."

"Yes, this Ewan…" Cade spat it as if it was a dirty word. "He smiles at her and is nice to her, and she might think he likes her and get all worked up, but a man won't commit to a widow with three young children. If he is interested, I would like to know what's behind it. His hidden agenda."

Lily suppressed a laugh. "Oh, Cade, you're so adorable when you get all protective. Gina doesn't need you to tell her that a man might have a hidden agenda. She is suspicious enough in her own right." Her amusement died, and she added with a sadness wringing inside, "Gina doesn't trust people anymore. And that is a bad thing. You can't live always expecting the worst. She must have faith again, in the future. We must encourage her to step out and try new things, not stand in her way."

Cade sighed. His frustration seemed to ebb away under the realization she was right. After a brief silence, he asked, "Do you think this center is a good place for her to be?"

"Well, at dinner I heard nice stories about Granny and Grizzly and fun things to do… It can't hurt to give it a try. Let Gina find out how she feels once she is making products and selling them. It will be hard work."

"Yes." Cade seemed to see a glimmer of hope. "Gina probably has a too-rosy view of running her own business. She is focused on the creative side of it, not the practical side, with paperwork and bills and unhappy customers."

"Why would her customers be unhappy?" Lily asked with a frown.

"You know how it goes. There are always folks who don't like something or wriggle to get a refund." Cade made a hand gesture. "Maybe those everyday struggles will convince her it's better to have a steady day job." Cade looked encouraged at the idea. "If she experiences the hurdles firsthand, it will work much better than if I tell her. I had never thought of it that way." He smiled at Lily. "What would I do without you?" He leaned down to kiss her.

Lily sank into the warmth of his embrace. It felt good to have come out of this discussion still holding on to each other.

But she wasn't quite calm below the surface. Because for the first time since they had married, they firmly disagreed on something. Cade wanted Gina to fail at selling her baked goods at the center and return to working a steady day job in town. But Lily didn't. She had a feeling the center would be good for Gina. She hoped with all of her heart that Gina would make a success of it and...find the happiness she craved.

CHAPTER NINE

"YES, IT IS that way." Gina pointed, and the family thanked her and moved on to the start of the adventure trail.

It was Gina's third weekend working at the center. She also came over on Wednesdays when there were school visits, and she really enjoyed working with the children who were all wide-eyed to see everything in and around the center. But Saturdays were just as busy and fulfilling with lots of families dropping by and Granny offering extra treats at the café.

Gina wiped a lock of hair from her face and exhaled for a moment as she recalled just how many pies and buns she had baked this week. It had been a race against the clock sometimes. But it gave her a satisfaction she had never had while still working for Bud at his Western store. She had to write him a card and tell him how happy she was now at the center.

Thank him, almost, for firing her?

She grinned to herself. That would be a bit much. But it was true. She couldn't imagine still selling boots and jackets. This seemed to be much nicer. Not in the least because of the wonderful people she had met here.

She heard Stacey's laughter and peeked into the playground where Grizzly was pushing the girls on the swings. He made sure Ann didn't go too high as she was easily frightened by speed, but Stacey couldn't go high enough, and Grizzly's roar of laughter mixed with her excited high-pitched giggles. Gina stood a moment watching her children play so contentedly, and she wondered when had been the last time she'd felt this sense of... Well, it was hard to tell what exactly it was. But she realized now that for a long time there had been an undercurrent of unrest in her life, of worry, over her situation and the question of whether it would ever be alright again. But now it seemed to be so much better. There was a sense of...having arrived.

She turned away and went inside the center, where Granny was busy changing the gift shop display cabinet. It was a task she jealously guarded and something she could spend hours on to get just right. Gina understood that to Granny this display represented her shop and all she had achieved at the center and that it was her pride and joy. It had to be wonderful to have created such a blooming business.

The door opened of the room where people could watch clips about the natural world surrounding them, and visitors poured out chatting among themselves. *Magnificent, impressive* were the recurring words. Gina smiled to herself. She had not yet found the time to go in there and watch the footage extensively. It seemed like a shame to hide in a dark room watching clips when you could also see it live outside the windows. It was great to be a part of this.

Then her ear caught another word. It was casually mixed into the jumble of comments as the group of people passed her. *Avalanche.*

No. She must have misheard. They wouldn't say *avalanche*. A cold feeling skittered across her back. Why would they say *avalanche*? That made no sense. She had mistaken some other word.

But still the ice settling in her stomach froze any happy feeling she'd had moments before. It was as if a dark cloud of anxiety descended upon the sunny landscape of her good mood, and she could feel a chilly breeze down her neck. Her husband was dead. How could she feel like everything was alright with the world?

She bit her lip and tried to take a deep breath. But her thoughts ran around in panicked circles. Was she such a bad woman for feeling joy again after her husband had died? For being happy that a coincidence—her boss's decision to leave town for a few months—had brought her here to a place...with mountains. The very natural phenomena she had vowed to hate. They were close. They were watching over this center. Not like a benign presence, a wonderful backdrop. No, they were towering over it. They were...

"Gina..." Ewan stood beside her. He had swept his sunglasses up on top of his head, and his face had this warm sun-kissed glow of having been outdoors all day long. His eyes shone at her with a kind invitation. "I have some time off until the next group wants their tour. How about a quick cup of coffee together?"

"Yes, that's fine." She said it automatically, her mind still fighting the uneasiness that had invaded her system upon hearing a single word. She was so easily unbalanced. But she should fight it. She had most certainly *not* heard the word *avalanche*. She should focus on the positive things she was experiencing here and how her work increased her sense of being independent and of outgrowing the shadows that had dominated her life for too long.

"Good." Ewan made an inviting gesture in the direction of the back room where the staff could have coffee and lunch. "It's great it's so busy early in the season. We normally see this kind of crowd only in summer. But I guess the center's website is working. We had someone overhaul the website and also make sure it's easier to find online. That it shows up on top in search results."

Gina nodded. "That's important."

Ewan continued enthusiastically, "We even got the website redone for free. Grizzly knew a man whose son had to design or rework a website from a real brand or business as part of getting his degree in marketing. He was really excited to work on our website because the Rockies have plenty of appeal, and his mentor was impressed that he had been able to get the job. It was a win-win."

They had arrived in the back room and went to the counter for coffee and tea. Gina grabbed a mug. Ewan said, "I thought you always wanted a bigger mug."

"Oh yes, but I didn't see it."

"Here, this is your usual mug, right?" Ewan

selected the white one with the ladybugs. He gave her a searching look. "You seem a bit distracted."

"Yes… I mean, no. I'm fine." She accepted the mug and reached out for the coffeepot. She wasn't about to share with him how a misheard word had upset her. He wouldn't understand. Ewan was so stable and practical. Sometimes she wondered whether anything ever got him angry or upset. She longed for a peek inside his mind. A look behind the friendly hospitality he showed to everyone.

Ewan frowned as he came to stand beside her with his own mug, a dark blue one with a tree silhouette in white. "Is something the matter? I know we are just colleagues, and we don't know each other well, perhaps, but… I do want to be there for you when you need someone to listen."

This might be the moment to share and get to know him better. Still, she didn't know if he would even get what she meant. Reluctantly, Gina shook her head. "There's nothing wrong. Just some silly misunderstanding."

"Having to do with your products?" he asked, filling his mug with coffee. "Your pie is a real winner with our guests. I can't imagine anyone not liking it."

"There are always people who don't like pie." Still, no one had complained or left a bad review on the center's website. That was promising. Gina felt an involuntary smile creep up. "You flatter me."

"No, I'm just telling the truth." Ewan took a sip of coffee, then added with a sincere look, "Like I'm telling the truth when I say I want to help you. That I'm here to listen if there is something weighing on your mind."

Now that he offered again, she really couldn't refuse. Actually, it might feel good to get it off her chest. Gina exhaled. "It's nothing. I was in a really good mood having seen the girls outside with Grizzly and… Then I was reminded of my husband, and I suddenly felt very sad. I guess it's natural."

EWAN LOOKED AT her pale face. The sadness in her eyes wrenched his heart. He wanted to make her smile again. But she was talking about the husband she had lost and… It was obvious she was still hurting. That she still… loved that man?

Of course she does, he told himself. *They were married for years; they had children together. She sees him in her baby boy. He even*

*has his father's name. That man will always
be a part of their lives, and that is only right.*

Still it gave him an uncomfortable feeling.
Almost as if…there was no room for him in
the equation?

That was odd. He was just a colleague, as he
had said himself. He could become a friend,
maybe. That was all. And he could be all that
without having to compete with Gina's de-
ceased husband.

A little embarrassed by his feelings, Ewan
walked away a few steps and took another sip
of coffee. This would have been hard with just
any person sharing her grief with him and his
not having a clue as how to respond. But now
it was extra painful. Because he wanted to say
all the right things, and he had no idea how to
handle this.

Eager for distraction, he searched his mind
for some nice lighthearted topic he could raise.
But suddenly he heard himself say, "How did
you meet anyway? You and your husband?"

Gina instantly smiled. Her eyes filled with
a tender glow. "That was very special. My
friends took me to an all-inclusive resort. Having been raised on a ranch in a small town, I'd
never been on vacation much, let alone gone
to a place like that. The luxury, the beautiful

rooms, the food put out in buffet style. It was all new to me, and where I had feared I would be like a fish out of water, struggling to make it through the day, I actually loved it from the moment I walked in. I felt like a princess. Really special and…different from what I usually was. There I met Barry. He had been to such places often. His parents ran a successful restaurant and…he was so suave. A real gentleman. I adored him from the moment I saw him. He looked so handsome in his suit when he came to dinner at night and…somehow he noticed me. I hadn't expected it. But apparently he also liked me. It was love at first sight for both of us."

Ewan nodded. It sounded like a scene from a movie. Something women wanted. A man who swept them off their feet with his good manners, well-chosen words and romantic gestures. The complete opposite of Ewan.

Gina continued, "We had candlelight dinners and walks along the beach, and we took trips to towns nearby. He bought me a necklace with a little silver star on it saying it was the star we could always wish on…" Her voice broke and tears filled her eyes.

Ewan stepped up to her, reaching out his hand to touch her arm. "I'm so sorry. I shouldn't have asked." He had to be the most insensitive man alive to have actually asked such a question. Why was he so badly versed in the social graces?

Gina shook her head. A tear leaked down her cheek. "No. It is good you asked. Too many people are afraid to ask. They don't want to touch on something painful, something hard. You see, that is what it is and will always remain. Hard. Loss is difficult, and it doesn't get easier over time. Sure, you learn how to cope with the practical side of it. Barry is no longer here so he can't pick up the girls from school or read to them when they go to bed. I have to do that or ask for others to help out with it. That can all be arranged for. But missing someone... Wishing he was still here..."

"No one can take his place, of course," Ewan said. *Especially because it seems he had it all: looks, money, a way with words. Everything a romantic woman like Gina craves. She loved him because he was her husband, of course, but also because he made her feel special.*

"It was my first real relationship," Gina said. "I fell in love and he loved me too, and we got engaged. We married. We had twins. It was all perfect. We were so happy and... It felt like it would never end. I guessed that I took it for granted sometimes. That I wasn't even aware how lucky I was. Until it all came crashing down around me. Because of one avalanche."

Ewan froze under the last word. He recalled Stacey's warning to him that Mom shouldn't see the images shown in their documentary. "Avalanche?" he repeated.

"Yes. Barry loved skiing. When we'd been together for a few months, we went on a trip together, but I never really got the hang of it. Like Ann, I'm not a fan of speed." She smiled through her tears. "Barry then created this tradition of going on a trip with friends. Every year in February. It was their guy thing, they used to say. They were all married or engaged, but on those trips they could be buddies again like they had been in college. Barry loved it. I was never excessively worried, although I disliked him being away and leaving me with the girls and the pizzeria. It was sometimes a lot to deal with on my own."

She sighed wistfully. "I had no idea then that very soon I would be doing it all alone, for the rest of my life."

"It doesn't need to be for the rest of your life," Ewan said softly. "I mean…"

She ignored him and continued, "On the last trip, two years ago, Barry had an accident.

They were caught unaware by an avalanche. All of his friends got away unscathed. He was the only one who…" She reached up and wiped a tear away with an impatient gesture. "It was so…unfair."

He watched as her expression contracted and she struggled to keep herself from breaking apart completely. He wanted to pull her into his embrace, but at the same time he didn't dare try. She was so vulnerable right now, and he didn't want to do anything to make her emotional turmoil worse.

"It's not that I wish the others had died as well," Gina said with difficulty. "I know they also had loved ones to go back to. But that is the thing. They were all able to go back and only Barry…" She hid her face in her hands and sobbed.

Ewan reached out and gently put his hand on her shoulder. He squeezed. "It's okay to feel that way, Gina. I mean, it would be strange if you hadn't thought so. Their families are still intact and yours was broken apart. You lost your husband. The girls lost their father. It must be hard for you to see their grief." He recalled Stacey's seriousness when she had told him that the cinema room was forbidden territory. She wanted to protect her mother and sister from pain. But seven-year-olds shouldn't have to think about such things. They should just play and be happy.

"I never knew your husband," he said gently. "But even I feel how unfair it is. That he should be torn away and never come back to you and never see his son. He never did see him, right? Considering how old Barry is…"

"Right." Gina lifted her face and looked him in the eye. Tears hung on her lashes. "I was pregnant with him when Barry had the accident. There I was all alone, left to take care of everything and… I just didn't know what to do. How to manage."

"But you did." Ewan held her gaze. "You did a wonderful job, Gina. Little Barry is a happy bouncing boy, and the twins are a pleasure to be around. You are raising a lovely little family. You can do this."

A hesitant smile broke the tension in her features. "You really think so?"

"Absolutely." He kept staring into her gorgeous eyes. The words came easily to him because she needed to hear them. "You can do anything you put your mind to. Make this business here a success and…"

The door opened and Grizzly came in with the girls. "Marshmallows!" he cried at the top of his voice and ran for a cupboard. The girls were all eyes for the promised treat and didn't notice their mother's state of mind. Gina quickly turned away, wiping at her smudged face. Ewan suddenly understood how often she had to go through this, deal with her grief alone to spare her children. It was great that she did so, but at the same time he wondered who was there for her, to help her get through this.

He said softly, "Take a moment for yourself. I'll distract the girls further."

He turned to Grizzly and the twins and said, "Ah, marshmallows. Are you sharing?"

"What do you think?" Grizzly asked, clutching the bag with a possessive intensity.

"He can have one," Stacey said generously.

"Just one?" Ewan asked, leaning down to her and giving her his most pleading look.

"Maybe two?" Ann ventured.

"Look at my size," Ewan said. "I'm three times as big as you are."

"No, you are not," Stacey protested. "If I stood on Ann's shoulders, we'd be taller than you."

"Really?" Ewan frowned as if he didn't believe it. "But in bulk… I am broader, you know."

From the corner of his eye, he saw Gina leave the room. He hoped she would be able to calm down and wash up before returning so the girls wouldn't notice a thing. It surprised him how protective he felt toward these little ones. They shouldn't feel any pain. They should have the kind of carefree childhood he himself had enjoyed.

But he knew that they would never have it. After all, Ewan had grown up with both his parents. There hadn't been any major loss in his life. He had only known the occasional heartache of having to move again or losing a beloved pet. But he had never suffered a big irrevocable loss like not having your father anymore. These girls were only seven. They would never have their father present at their graduation or to give them away at their wedding. They would always feel that void. It hurt him deep inside, and he wanted to do something about it. Take the pain away if he could. But he couldn't. Gina should meet a man like her husband had been, who could give her that romantic fantasy all over. What use was a loner to her, an outdoor man who lacked social graces, who lived in a simple cabin, who worked in the mountains that represented the essence of her grief?

He was of the mountains, and she was of the valley. That was right, wasn't it? They were just poles apart.

Gina stood in the ladies' room and washed her face. She was so thankful there wasn't anyone else there. But considering how busy it was, someone could come in at any moment. So she hurried to dry her face with a paper towel and practiced a wide smile in front of the mirror. It looked…pretty good.

Actually, she realized, she felt better now that she had cried. Or was it because Ewan had talked to her in a way few other people ever had? He hadn't tried to smooth over rough edges or say it would get better. No. He had acknowledged the pain and been there for her. He had even said she was doing a good job with her family. He had said it plainly and therefore she believed him. She could never stand long-winded compliments or complicated explanations. Ewan was someone who spoke his mind. Or maybe he spoke what was in his heart. And he had a good heart.

Gina stared into her own eyes for a few moments. Ewan was important to her. More than just a colleague, someone she met here at the center, who was kind to her and helped with the twins. He was becoming a friend, or…whatever word she could fit to the feeling she had inside for him. A feeling that was just showing itself carefully like a little flower sticking its head out from under the winter snow.

The snow she hated so much. But it was melting. And it was making way for something new. Something special.

The door opened, and a mother and daughter came in. Gina smiled at them and left the room. She felt a little caught out, not by their arrival but by her own feelings. She wasn't quite sure why but...

"Ah, Gina!" Granny waved at her from the counter of the gift shop area. A tall well-dressed man stood there with a full head of graying hair. As Gina walked over, his imposing figure struck a bit of awe in her like the school principal always had.

Granny said to the man, "This is Mrs. Gina Williams. Gina, this is Mr. Wilcox. He runs several large restaurants in Yewcreek and along the highway. He is very impressed with our apple pie."

"You see, Mrs. Williams," Mr. Wilcox said, taking Gina's hand in his, "it is hard to find good apple pie for my restaurants. Often the dough is too sticky or the apple is mashed and the whole pie feels like a cheap product. But the pie here, the pie that you baked as I understood from Mrs. Grant here, is delicious. It has the perfect amount of raisins and that subtle hint of cinnamon. I want it in my restaurants. I would love to do business with you."

"But I am just a one-woman business," Gina said blinking.

"Well, my dear lady, I wanted to suggest a small start. I have a wedding party coming to Yewcreek next Saturday. Two hundred people. Now instead of a conventional wedding cake, they want apple pies because apples played a big part in their love story."

Thinking of her parents' orchard and how happy they had been together, Gina had to smile. "That sounds wonderful."

"You make the pies and have them delivered to my restaurant. If they like them and all works well, logistically, we can do more business. What do you say?"

"I think it's a great idea," Granny enthused. She gave Gina a subtle nod to indicate she should accept.

Gina hesitated a moment. That the bride and groom's love story involved apples was very special. Almost like it was meant to be. Why not take this assignment and test herself? If she could actually do this, she could do more. Taking a deep breath, she said, "I would love to work with you."

"Good, good. If you write down your contact information, including email, I will send you a simple contract so we are all agreed on what to expect of each other." Mr. Wilcox smiled at her. "My wife is waiting for me outside to take a little tour. When we come back, I will pick up the information from this lady here." He gestured at Granny. "Thank you. Goodbye."

He walked to the door. Gina saw him meet up with Ewan. Apparently he was taking these people out on the tour. Her gaze lingered a moment on Ewan's dark head as he walked out. She hadn't even properly thanked him for being so kind to her when she had cried.

"What do you think of that?" Granny whispered to her. "Isn't it an amazing opportunity? When he praised the apple pie to me, I knew I had to mention your name and explain you live on a ranch with an apple orchard. He was immediately interested in the local connection. Isn't this wonderful?" She clapped her hands together. "You will become a sensation at that wedding."

"But two hundred guests... I'll need thirty pies. At least. People do take second servings, you know."

"Especially of your apple pie." Granny

pinched her arm. "Isn't this just perfect? I knew it would be a good idea for you to come and work here."

Gina exhaled slowly. The prospect of having to bake that many pies was daunting. After all, Mr. Wilcox expected them all to have that wonderful subtle hint of cinnamon and... What else had he said? Her head swam.

"Mommy." Ann popped up and pulled her arm. "Can we go into the garden? Do you have time to take us? I want to smell the plants again."

"Go," Granny said. "Take a little time for the girls. It's getting quieter as the afternoon winds down. I'll manage."

"Really?" Gina asked.

"Of course." Granny waved a hand. "Go now and have fun."

Gina took a girl on each hand and walked outside. The air was fresh, the sun shone down on them and she felt like she was stepping into a whole new beginning. Her own baking business... Could it really take off? Would it become much more than the occasional project in town? Could she really provide for her family?

She had to have faith in her own abilities. After all, Ewan had said that she did a wonderful job. And he was an honest man. She could believe him.

CHAPTER TEN

"I NEVER THOUGHT I would get so stressed out from baking." Gina rubbed her arm over her forehead because her hands were stuck in oven mitts to take the last load of apple pies from the oven. "It was always fun to do. But now I'm not sure it's any good."

She threw a desperate look at the kitchen table, which was full of baked pies. Her mother and Lily were busy putting pies in plastic boxes for transport. As Yewcreek was quite a drive, Gina had agreed to let a friend of Cade's take them in his truck. He was leaving town at 5:00 a.m. to go to a cattle auction and would deliver the pies first, ensuring they were there early for the festivities.

Lily said, "They look and smell delicious."

"But we haven't tasted them," Gina said. "I feel like I should take a bite out of each one to make sure they taste right."

"That would look a bit odd," her mother said

dryly and they all laughed. Gina was the first to get serious again. "Honestly, Mom, what if I flunk this? I invested in buying all the ingredients and in these transport boxes and the extra fridge to keep it all cool and... I don't know. Maybe I shouldn't have taken this offer..." What had gotten into her to suddenly want to be independent? It had felt wonderfully adventurous, but now she was just bone weary and so insecure.

Her mother shook her head with a frown. "Why all the worries, Gina? We think you make the best pie in the county, possibly in the state. High time others came to the same conclusion."

Gina nodded agreement. She was tired now but that would pass. She should be proud of herself that she had actually baked all these pies. That she had made the deadline. That her pies would be a part of a wonderful wedding tomorrow. It felt special to contribute to the couple's happiness. To be involved in a local event. It could be good for business too. Who knew, others might offer her opportunities. Her fledgling business could really take off after tomorrow. That was exciting.

Daunting and exciting, all rolled into one.

Her phone rang, and she struggled to get a

mitt off to take the call. It was Ewan. "How is the baking going?" he asked.

Just hearing his voice made the scale tip to exciting rather than daunting. After all, Ewan had supported the plan wholeheartedly, had even offered to take the pies to Yewcreek for her. But she knew he also had to give tours at the center on Saturday and didn't want him to get up so early and make a long round trip ahead of his normal duties.

"I just took the last two from the oven." A sense of accomplishment filled her. She should be proud of what she was doing here.

"Congratulations."

"I can't taste them and… I'm suddenly worried I made a mistake. Not enough flour, too much sugar. Or the apples could be very sour." She stared hard at the pies as if to see into them and determine whether they had any fatal flaws.

"I'm sure they are just fine. Don't worry. Listen, I wanted to ask you if you have time to come to the center a little early tomorrow morning and help me check the adventure trail. We do these checks every few weeks to make sure it still functions as it should."

Gina took a deep breath. Her shoulders ached and she was ready for a long night in bed. But she had to get up early to hand the pies to the man delivering them, and after that she wouldn't get a wink of sleep, stressing about their arrival and Mr. Wilcox's opinion. Maybe meeting Ewan at the center early was just the answer. "Okay," she said, "what time? I'll be up early anyway to hand over the pies."

"How about seven? I know it's very early but… We have to be done before the first visitors arrive."

"Okay, fine with me." She felt a little better knowing she would have something to do tomorrow, other than agonizing about her pies. "Thanks, Ewan."

"What for?" She heard the smile in his voice. "See you tomorrow."

She disconnected and turned to her mother and Lily, who were walking around the table looking at all the pies. "They look so uniform," Mom enthused. "Really professional."

"I hope Mr. Wilcox feels the same way," Gina said with a sigh. She heard Barry gurgle in his playpen and went to pick him up. He immediately examined the one mitt she was still wearing.

"Maybe he wants to be a baker too," Lily suggested with a wink. They all laughed.

EWAN PACED UP and down the parking lot, waiting for Gina to arrive. At first Fuzzy had joined him, but after the fifth time she had gone to sit beside a tree trunk watching him as if she wasn't quite sure what he was up to.

"I hope it will work out great," he said to Fuzzy. "Gina deserves a pat on the shoulder, you know. If this Mr. Wilcox praises her, she will believe him. I'm not sure she believes me."

He stood a moment staring at the dirt in front of his feet. Had he laid it on too thick saying she did great with her kids? It was the truth, but maybe she had thought he was just trying to make her feel better because she had cried. He had gone over the scene a few times in his mind wondering if he could have done better. He also did that with rescues, reevaluating what had gone well and what could be better. There were always improvements to make…

But dealing with Gina's grief wasn't a job he could do well or badly. It was a personal thing and… It mattered a lot how he did.

Maybe more than he cared to admit to himself.

He knew he wasn't a people person, and he had little experience dealing with situations where people confided in him about personal issues. Still, it felt like he had done the right thing. With Stacey too when she had been sad.

He had just known what to say. Without training, without instructions. It was strange. But
amazing. This little family was something special, changing his life around.

A car engine sounded and Gina's station
wagon pulled into the lot. Ewan exhaled and
rushed to meet her. Fuzzy ran after him, eager
to say hello.

Gina clambered out of the car and leaned
down to pat Fuzzy. "Hello there, how are you?
What a beautiful morning." She straightened
up and looked Ewan in the eye. "Hello."

He stared into her eyes a moment not knowing what to say.

*Hello maybe? Good morning? Some other
greeting?*

"How did things go with the pies?" he asked.
That got her talking at once.

"Oh, just great. Cade's friend picked them
up, they all fitted in the back of the truck, and
he drove off so…" She pulled her phone from
her pocket and looked at the screen. "The odd
thing is that he should have delivered them to
Mr. Wilcox by now, but I haven't had a message from him yet. What if he doesn't like
them?"

Ewan put his hand on her arm. "He'll like

them. Come on. Let's get on the trail to check all the family attractions."

Gina fell into step beside him. The early sunlight caressed the blond locks dangling across her shoulders. She looked so pretty. But that would be totally weird to say. Off the bat, out of the blue… They were colleagues. Friends maybe. But friends didn't say such things.

"What exactly are we checking?" she asked.

"Well, the trail has several features like logs to climb on, a little hut kids can get into, plaques with information, a forest phone…"

"What is a forest phone?" Gina asked.

"Wait and see." Ewan put his hands in his pockets as he walked. Being here in the quiet sun-streaked forest calmed the turmoil inside, the feeling he didn't understand what was happening, that he was losing control. He looked about him, enjoying all the shades of green and the birdsong echoing from the treetops. "This is just perfect."

"What is? Keeping me in suspense?"

"Being here. In the forest. With no other people around. You know?"

"You are really in your element here."

"Yes, sometimes I don't get it myself. I could have lived anywhere really. The desert, the jungle." As he spoke, he saw scenes from the travels with his parents, felt the dry heat and the sand that got everywhere, heard the calls of tropical birds overhead and the splash of his dad's canoe paddle in the river.

"Desert, jungle?" Gina looked confused.

He realized he had never told her about his childhood, and she probably wondered what on earth he meant. "I was raised by two world travelers who lived off grid in the wilderness. Extreme environments often. Hot, cold. With snakes and scorpions and predators."

"Oh." She looked startled.

He rushed to say, "It wasn't really that dangerous. My parents took good care of me. I mean, you have animals on the ranch too. They can bite or kick if you upset them. You teach your children how to be safe around them. So my parents taught me how to look out for snakes and predators and what to do when under attack."

"It's not quite the same thing," Gina said.

Ewan suppressed a smile. "At the heart of it, it is," he said with a glance at her. "You raise children to become independent human beings that can take care of themselves. You teach them everything they need to know to make it in the world. Whether it is the urban world or an outdoor environment. It's all a matter of skills."

GINA WASN'T TOO SURE. She bet that if Barry had lived, he'd have wanted to teach the girls how to ski. But then they would have been on the slopes with him, and an avalanche could have grabbed them as well. You had to protect children against harm. Keep them in a safe zone.

"It's important to know about the world you are living in," Ewan said quietly. "Admire it but also know the dangers and the limitations you face." He looked around him. "It is safer here than in many places I visited as a child and a teenager. Maybe that's why I sometimes wonder why I like this so much."

"You're a thrill seeker," Gina suggested with a chill inside. How wrong she had been about him! She had envisioned him having been raised in the city, having embraced nature as a way to escape all the concrete. But he had been raised in the jungle and the desert—places she couldn't even imagine visiting. And raising children there? Impossible. They were really so different.

"No, not at all," Ewan responded quietly to her question. "But because we traveled so much and my parents were always on the move, I kind of expected to love that lifestyle as well. To want to see places and have new experiences. I never thought I would have a cabin in a North American forest and go to a day job and…feel happy." He looked at her and smiled. "It goes to show that things turn out differently than you expect."

She nodded. The idea that he had settled here was nice. But a cabin in the forest was hardly her idea of a family home. She envisioned something close to Heartmont, where her family and friends were, where she was just starting to build her business. She had once followed a man into his world, and it had ended in heartbreak. She wasn't going to follow anyone anymore.

"Here we are at the first attraction." Ewan stopped and pointed at tree trunks that had different heights. Fuzzy walked around them, sniffing the wood.

Ewan explained, "Kids must jump from one to the other. We have to make sure they are still firmly attached to the forest floor. So, how about you jump from one to the other and test it?"

She bet that he wanted her to protest, but Gina had always been good at things that demanded balance, so she nodded and hopped onto the first tree trunk. She was taller, of course, than kids were, so it was rather easy to hop from one to the other. Fuzzy yapped as if she was encouraging her.

Ewan stayed close by as if he thought she might lose her balance and…would have to be caught?

For a moment she imagined him reaching out and catching her… How would it feel to be in his arms?

Her cheeks heated. She shouldn't fantasize about something that would never happen. Even if she was attracted to him, she wouldn't allow any closeness between them. They were colleagues and had to work together. She had to make sure this stayed strictly professional.

Ewan said, "Is it going okay?"

"Sure. These are fine." She jumped down from the last one in a hurry and put her hands in her pockets. She felt unnerved and jittery, like she was back in high school. She should never have agreed to do this early morning check. Being together felt so…right. But that was just a silly feeling. The reality was that they were very different and would never want the same things.

Ewan nodded. "Good, then we can move on to the next. You are really light on your feet, just like a deer."

From a ranger like Ewan, that was probably

a compliment. She suppressed a laugh. They followed the path to the next attraction, the little hut he had mentioned. Kids could go in via the door and look out the window. There were a few pebbles on the windowsill, suggesting some kids had played pretend here. Maybe they imagined that this was an ice cream window and the customers bought their cones with pebble money? Having enough experience watching the girls turn anything into an opportunity for role-play, Gina could readily imagine it.

"You are better suited to fit inside," Ewan said.

Gina raised an eyebrow. "You really expect me to crawl in there?"

"Nah. The roof looks sturdy enough." He slapped on it with a flat hand. "So we can move on."

"I can do it, of course," Gina said, suddenly eager to prove herself. She crawled in through the door. Fuzzy tried to get in after her, but Ewan called the dog to him.

Gina sat inside, bent forward and stuck her head out the window. "Hello."

Ewan sat on his haunches in front of the window. "Hello." As she looked into his eyes, it struck her how this was almost like a thing couples did, when they were frolicking and having fun together. She had forgotten how that was. It seemed so long ago.

Her face was on fire now, and she crawled backward, hitting her head on the doorpost.

"Are you okay?" Ewan asked.

"Yeah, fine." She straightened up and redid her hair, brushed off her clothes. She was a grown woman, a mother of three, no less. She shouldn't forget her dignity. Or her responsibilities. She wasn't a teenager who could... fall in love?

"Ah, you wondered what a forest phone was, right?" Ewan asked. "We will be there in a moment."

"Well, whatever it is, I did my share of the checking, now it's your turn," she rushed to say.

Ewan looked at her. "I will need your help with this one. It takes two to make it work."

It takes two to make it work. Marriage did. Friendships did. Lots of things that were worth it took two people. To lessen the load or lend a hand. It was different on your own. Harder.

A whole lot harder.

She swallowed as she followed him to a long tree trunk that lay flat, supported on beams so it was off the ground. It had a thing attached that looked like a funnel. Even Fuzzy seemed to give it a bewildered look as if, like Gina, she wasn't sure what it was.

"I will stand over there…" Ewan pointed at the other end of the log that also had a device attached. "I will say something, and you can hear it on your end. It functions like the whispering gallery in old houses."

"Ah." Gina nodded. She leaned over and held her ear to the funnel.

It took a moment before she heard anything but the soft breath of the wind and the birdsong. Then she heard a voice saying, *You look so pretty.*

Uh… Could that be right? She didn't dare look at him. She kept leaning into the thing, listening. Again, she heard *You look so pretty.*

"And?" Ewan called out to her.

"I can't make it out. Something about the light being pretty?" She was sure she looked like a tomato right now. Fortunately her phone beeped. Finally. Mr. Wilcox about the pies!

She grabbed the phone from her pocket and checked the message. It was a photo of some transport boxes. Because they were transparent, Gina could see inside. Her heart stopped, then thundered on. The apple pies inside had slid to a side and were crumbled. One had even broken open, apple spilling out. The accompanying text read, "I am sure this is not how you handed them out to your deliveryman. But he goofed. This cannot be served to my guests. I won't be able to pay for this."

Gina stood there staring at the photo. She should never ever have let someone else deliver her pies. No matter how long the drive, she should have done it herself. Now Mr. Wilcox wasn't paying. She had lost all of her investments. In the ingredients, the transport boxes, the extra fridge.

"What's wrong?" Ewan's voice asked from nearby.

She looked up into his friendly face. "The pies… I don't understand how, but during transport they were damaged. Mr. Wilcox can't use them for the wedding party. I won't be paid."

No money, her internal voice sang in her head. *You knew it was a risk. Cade warned you. What will he say when he finds out? How can you face him tonight?*

Ewan gently pulled the phone from her hand and looked at the photo. "I see five damaged pies. What about the rest? You told me you were making over thirty?"

"I did. I guess they were all damaged?"

"How?" Ewan held her gaze. "These look

like someone let them slide. Did it happen on the drive? Are they all damaged? Or was it an accident carrying them in? Are there good ones left?"

"He is receiving two hundred people."

"Yes, but he can't simply say he won't pay for all the pies. Why don't you call him and ask what happened?"

His suggestion made her angry. As if she didn't know she should do that. She had run a successful pizzeria, she had dealt with unhappy customers before. But this was her very first assignment for her own business. It was her on her own now, without Barry having her back. She felt so completely exposed, not ready to take the brunt of Wilcox's disappointment in her. Still, she snapped at Ewan, "I know what to do, without you telling me."

"Okay." He stepped back. "Then make the call. I'll wait for you down the path."

As he walked away, she took a deep breath and rehearsed what she was going to say to Wilcox. *You have to know if the whole load is damaged. You have to be strong and deal with this like a business owner would. Call the man.*

Better still, call Cade's friend first and ask him what happened.

She placed the call and waited for the answer. Cade's friend sounded far off, and there was a lot of accompanying noise. He had to be at the auction already. "What happened to the pies? Did you drop some?"

"Yeah, like four maybe? Sorry about that. I was in a hurry to get back on the road again. I'm no delivery boy, you know."

"Just four? Not all of them?"

"Nope, just four."

"Thanks." She disconnected. Now that she knew the full story, a bit of frustration crept up. Mr. Wilcox had a nerve to send her a photo of four damaged pies and tell her he wasn't paying her. He had a right to a discount because four pies had been damaged, but he couldn't simply state he was not paying at all. But she had to suppress her irritation and handle this professionally. She placed a new call and hopped up and down nervously as she waited for him to answer.

"Wilcox." It sounded curt and agitated. "I am very busy right now, Mrs. Williams. I have a wedding party arriving and nothing is done right."

"I'm sorry that the man who delivered the pies dropped a few. But you still have thirty-one pies that you can use. I am sure it will be enough for your guests. I won't charge for the damaged pies, of course." This sounded very reasonable to her own ears, and she was proud of herself for offering this solution that served both parties.

"You haven't read our contract, have you?" His voice was lined with ice. "It says that a delivery needs to be unblemished. That goes for all parts of it. If a part isn't perfect, the deal is off. You get nothing. Sorry, but I have learned the hard way to do business like that. People are sloppy. They don't care about my reputation."

"I'm not responsible for the actions of my deliveryman. I mean, I never meant for him to drop the pies and ruin all my hard work." Gina caught the note of desperation in her own voice. She closed her eyes a moment. This wasn't going to convince him he was dealing with a solid business partner. But then again, what could convince him? He sounded dead set in his view of the situation.

Wilcox said, "I'm sorry but I must have the same rules for everyone. No money and that's final." He disconnected without even saying goodbye.

Gina took a deep breath. Her head was spinning, and her mouth was dry. She clutched the phone as if willpower could still make a change. He had to understand her position, he had to…

But apparently he didn't. Her first assignment had gone spectacularly wrong. She had made a crucial mistake signing that contract without thinking through what it meant. How a flaw in even one pie would discredit the whole delivery. How had she missed that? Where was her head for business?

Then again, Barry had always dealt with paperwork and finances.

Which was why she hadn't known about the debts until it was too late.

"Hey." Ewan stood beside her, eyeing her worriedly. "I am sorry if I was curt with you. But you have to be businesslike about this. He isn't doing you a favor. This is about a serious endeavor."

"Which went seriously awry. I guess I should never have taken this so-called wonderful offer." She swallowed down a lump in her throat. Time to confess to Ewan what she had done. "And I should have read his contract better. Then I would have known that even the slightest error could trip me up." She told him what Wilcox had said.

Ewan frowned. "Do you still have more pies at home?"

"Yes, I baked a few extra just in case."

"Great. If I deliver four new pies to him, before the wedding party needs them, will he pay you?"

"I don't know. But, Ewan, that is madness. You'd have to get them at the ranch, drive to Yewcreek... You have work to do here. You are booked for tours. If anyone has to solve this mess, it's me."

"But you are shaken by the situation. If you go, you might get into an argument with Wilcox. I'm not personally involved and will be perfectly civil to him. The new pies will smooth things over and your business prospects will be fine." Ewan checked his watch. "I can make it if I start out right away. Unless you think I will also drop your pies?" He winked at her.

She almost had to smile. "No, I don't think you'd do that. And you're right about the way I feel. I would never be able to keep my face blank. He would sense my frustration from a mile off. I'll call to make sure he will accept this solution."

Gina called the number again. Wilcox answered with a "Look, Mrs. Williams, if you are planning to plead with me, there is no point to it. I have a guy here with a gazebo that doesn't fit because he brought the wrong size. I have far more important things to do than argue with..."

"I can get you four new pies. Will you pay me then?"

"Homemade like the others? Not store-bought?"

"No, homemade from the same batch."

"You're on. But you have to be here before ten."

"That's a deal." Gina disconnected and looked at Ewan. "He will take them if he gets them before ten o'clock."

"Good. You can stay here and help Granny, and ask Grizzly to take any groups that turn up before I'm back." Ewan rushed down the path, and Gina ran after him. "You will be careful, won't you? Don't hurry so much that you get into trouble."

"I won't."

In the parking lot he gave her Fuzzy's leash. The dog pushed herself against Gina's leg as if she knew she had to stay with her now. Ewan said, "Don't worry. We'll make it work."

She looked into his eyes, and she knew he meant it. He was doing this especially for her.

"Thanks, Ewan." She put her hand on his shoulder, stood on tiptoe and kissed him on the cheek. His aftershave swirled around her, filled her head with a spicy masculine scent.

She stepped back, and he dived into his car to leave. Her head still spun with all that had happened so quickly, and her heart beat fast with worry that they would somehow not make the deadline and lose the money anyway. Was it even smart to try and make it right?

But Ewan wanted to try for her sake and… he was truly special.

EWAN SPENT HIS drive to Yewcreek rehearsing what he would say to Mr. Wilcox. He might have claimed that he wasn't personally involved and would be perfectly civil, but with every mile he came closer to his destination, he realized more how wrong he had been there. He was personally involved and he didn't feel like being civil at all. Actually, thinking about how sad she had looked and how she had suddenly doubted all of her abilities, he was angry. Angry enough to give the man a piece of his mind.

But in his line of work, Ewan had learned quickly to keep emotions out of the way. Sometimes when he heard how people had gone missing in the mountains, he couldn't believe how naive they were in not following paths or not taking along food and drink, or going out when the weather forecast was bad. But people who didn't know the dangers of the terrain did such things, and his getting worked up about it served no purpose. In those circumstances he had to keep a clear head and do what was best for them. Because he was the professional.

Likewise, in this moment, he had to think of the best way to speak to Wilcox so Gina's reputation would be saved and her business wouldn't suffer from this unfortunate incident. Maybe Wilcox wasn't even the guilty party. It had been Cade's friend who'd brought the pies to the restaurant who had dropped them. It was a combination of things that had led to Gina being blamed for the whole failure. But that wasn't going to stay that way. Not if Ewan could help it.

He took a deep breath. He might tell himself that this was like so many situations he had to deal with, but it didn't feel that way. The term "personally involved" seemed to gain new meaning. This wasn't about chipping in for a colleague or a friend, smoothing over some difficulties as an impartial outsider. He felt like he had an actual stake in all of this. He wanted to see Gina smile again. He wanted her to believe in her own capabilities. He wanted her to be able to provide for her little family. Meeting her and the girls, little Barry, had opened up new layers of emotions inside him. Even a need to…belong?

A need to no longer be on his own, doing what he wanted, but part of their circle, doing what was right for them, helping them…

He caught himself talking out loud, going through various scenarios from being reasonable with Wilcox and saying he fully understood how he felt, to making him see that it hadn't really been Gina's fault at all but that of the man who had delivered the pies. Finally, before he was decided on the best course of action, the restaurant came into sight and he turned into the parking lot. There were several vans there with names like Ken's Catering and Gazebo Rental and as he got the pies from the back of his vehicle, he could already hear excited voices. A tall man with a full head of graying hair was shouting at a young man with ginger hair who stood beside a half-built gazebo. Another man, with dark curls, was just going inside the restaurant carrying boxes.

Ewan walked up to the older man and asked, "Mr. Wilcox?"

The man shot him an agitated look. "What do you want? Oh…" His gaze fell to the boxes with pies. "Yes, the replacement delivery. Well, they'd better be homemade pies, not bought in the supermarket, to satisfy me and get paid."

Ewan opened his mouth to explain that Gina was an honest woman who would never dupe her customers, but the man had already turned back to the gazebo builder. Ewan sighed and carried his load inside.

In the hallway of the restaurant, the man with the boxes was in a discussion with a waiter about where something had to be put. Judging by their raised voices, they weren't agreed on the place. Ewan decided not to ask where he had to go but figure it out for himself. He turned left and entered a large room where tables were set up. The decorations were all in red and white, but there seemed to be something missing. After a good look around, he realized what it was. Flowers. Usually at such festive occasions there would bouquets on tables and to decorate the platform where the happy couple sat, but there were none in sight. Hadn't they asked for any?

He went back into the hallway where the discussion was ongoing and turned left to find the kitchen. Having passed through another large room he found it and delivered the pies to the man in a white apron who was rushing around. "Oh, this is good," he said with a relieved look. "Now we have enough to make it work. The apple pies are so important for the big day. Our couple met in an orchard. They were both apple pickers. They asked to have the best apple pie in the region for their big day." He smiled at Ewan. "Having tasted Mrs. Williams's creations before, I can vouch she is truly a gifted baker."

Ewan felt a bit of tension relax. "She is," he agreed. "I hope it will be a beautiful day for the couple."

The cook sighed. "I doubt it. Mr. Wilcox has been preparing all of this for weeks to make it memorable. The groom is the son of one of his closest friends. This means so much to him. To have them celebrate here, at his restaurant. But everything seems to be conspiring against him. The pies were dropped, and the flowers haven't arrived yet."

"They haven't?" Ewan asked, remembering the barren room.

"The delivery van has a flat tire. The driver doesn't know how to change it, and he has to wait for help. But it is not easy to get roadside assistance on a Saturday."

"Is he stranded far from here?"

"Twelve miles. Mr. Wilcox would have

driven out himself to get the flowers, but they need to be transported in that van or they might get damaged. And he can't change a tire either. He is very frustrated."

"I can understand." Ewan came to a quick decision. The fate of this wedding was really none of his business and he had little time, but he could lend a hand and maybe mollify Wilcox so he would be nicer to Gina. Seeing her smile was worth it. "I can change tires on whatever vehicle. I can drive out there and help. Could you give me the exact location?"

The cook was happy to oblige, and Ewan left with the information in his phone. He passed Wilcox and the gazebo builder. The first was still arguing, while the latter stood with his head down, mortified, judging by his high color.

Ewan stopped to ask, "What seems to be the problem here?"

"I ordered a tent online," Wilcox said, apparently eager to make his point once more. "I entered the exact measurements for it to fit here in this space. Now they sent me the wrong tent. How will I ever explain to my guests that we don't have a party tent?"

Ewan looked at the unhappy young man and asked, "Is it too large?"

The young man nodded without a word.

Wilcox said, "Don't bother telling me that we might turn it because we have already discussed that option and it won't work. There is simply not enough space here."

"And how about on the other side of the building?" Ewan pointed to where he saw some open space.

Wilcox blinked. "On the other side of the building?" he repeated as if he suddenly became aware there even was another side to the building. "But that isn't convenient. My entrance is on this side."

"Yes, but you have a room there and the glass doors of that room open onto that space."

Wilcox stared at him. "But we aren't using that room. I put everything ready in the other room. The tablecloths, the cutlery."

"But the flowers aren't here yet," Ewan said. "You better see if the gazebo fits there and if it does, change the rooms around, because the flowers will be here soon and then you have to know where to put them. See you later." And he walked off.

He bet that if he had bothered to look back, Wilcox would have stared after him with his mouth open. It almost made him laugh. It felt good to help out. He liked that. And with a little luck, Gina would get her money.

AT THE CENTER, Gina was waiting anxiously for Ewan's return. He had things to do, people to show around, and it wasn't right that he was away on her business and would miss his own tours. She should never have accepted his offer. She should have gone to Wilcox herself, even if he would have noticed her mood and it would have soured relations between them even further. She bet her chance to deliver pies to his restaurants was ruined anyway.

She paced up and down, feeling her heart-beat flutter in her throat.

Granny gave her a sideways glance. "Don't worry, honey. Ewan will make it work. He is used to solving sticky situations." She chuckled at her own joke. "Pie, sticky, you get it?"

Gina wasn't in the mood for wordplay. "I shouldn't have let him go. It was a nice offer, but pointless anyway. Wilcox was so angry. He won't even want my pies anymore. I bet he is on the phone right now ordering different ones from a professional baker, not someone who makes a few pies in the kitchen of her own home." After a deep breath, she added,

"Which isn't even my own home but my family's home."

Granny frowned at her. "Does it bother you so much to live with them? I bet they love you, and it's nice for the girls to have their grandmother and uncle and auntie so close."

"Sure." Gina nodded. She felt her cheeks heat under Granny's scrutiny. "I don't want to seem ungrateful. But sometimes I wish I had my own place. It feels a little…dependent to live with my family. Like I can't take care of my own life."

"Is that how you feel or how others make you feel?" Granny came to stand close to her and said softly, "I understand, Gina. I became a widow when I was just thirty-five. I had loved my husband since I was fifteen. We were high school sweethearts. It felt like my whole life had been taken away from me. But after a year or so people started to say I should find myself a new husband. I wasn't getting any younger, they argued, and if I still wanted children… My husband and I never had any. It was the only shadow on our great happiness." She stared into the distance a moment. "I wasn't ready to date. I missed him. I have always kept on missing him."

Gina's throat constricted. She understood

completely. At the oddest moments she could, without warning, feel that pang of pain and longing, that ache for Barry to walk through the door and sweep her into his embrace. For her to feel safe again, like she had when he was alive.

But Granny didn't know one thing. How their situations differed. Granny had lost the love of her life, and she had felt uprooted and lost. Gina had lost the man she had loved more than anything, but she had also discovered right after his death that he had kept secrets from her. The debts that had destroyed her life, taken everything away from her. The pizzeria that Barry's parents had entrusted to them, the house they had been so happy in.

Everything they had had together, to which her memories were attached, had been lost. As if her entire life with Barry had been erased. It had been incredibly hard, and on top of her grief and loss she had also felt anger at him. She'd wanted to know why he had acted the way he had, endangering their little family, but she hadn't been able to ask. She'd been left with so many questions that had changed the way she felt about him and their marriage.

Granny said, "I can understand that you don't need people to interfere in your life,

Gina. To tell you how to deal with your situation or what is best for you. You have to decide that for yourself. I hope you will make all the right decisions and find happiness for yourself and the children." She squeezed Gina's arm. "You have friends here who will support you, regardless of what you decide to do."

Gina nodded. She shouldn't decide anything right now. Emotional turmoil wasn't the right base for a solid view of her future. Baking gave her so much joy. She wanted to continue with it. With or without Mr. Wilcox as a customer. Yes, her budget had taken a dent. But she could make it. Wilcox's interest had shown her her pies were restaurant-worthy. Why not find other takers? Why not continue on the path of building her business and dreaming about a place of her own? A cute little house in town, close to all facilities, where she could easily bake and deliver her goodies. A wonderful future for her little family.

All by yourself? a voice inside questioned.

For a moment she recalled the sweetness of her goodbye to Ewan, the kiss on his cheek, the tenderness in his eyes as he had looked at her before walking away.

Her breath caught. Ewan was beginning to mean a lot to her.

Maybe too much?

That could be way more dangerous to her dreams of a rosy future than any canceled order ever could.

WHEN EWAN CAME back to the restaurant, following the man in the flower van with the fixed tire, he saw at once that the gazebo had been set up on the other side of the building. It fit there and looked inviting in the cheerful sunshine.

Good. Wilcox was frustrated but he still saw reason. They could make this work.

Ewan got out and helped the flower man carry the first buckets with blooms inside. "This way," he told him, walking ahead to the room that opened onto the gazebo. Wilcox was putting a few last items in place on a table in the corner. When he saw Ewan with the buckets of flowers, his expression lit. "You really did it. Cook said you were going to fix the tire, but I didn't think… You did it!" He quickly came over and checked the flowers. They were also in red and white like the other decorations. "Perfect. Just perfect." He checked his watch. "If we get them spread around fast, we can still make it."

While the flower deliveryman and the cook

and another helper set to work, Wilcox looked at Ewan. "I don't know how to thank you. In fact... I don't know why you wanted to help. I..." He hesitated a moment and then pushed on firmly, "I behaved in a very bad manner. I was so unkind to Mrs. Williams. I told her that I wasn't going to pay her at all because of four broken pies. I made a contract with her, yes, and to make a thing like this work, I need a complete shipment or else...but still... I could have been friendlier. I...was just so frustrated about everything going wrong at once. The gazebo didn't fit, the flowers would be late and...then that guy dropping four pies. It was too much."

"I can understand. Your cook told me this wedding is very special to you because it concerns someone very dear."

Wilcox nodded. "I want everything to be perfect for them, to show how happy I am for them. They both lost their spouse and thought they would never marry again. But now they are, and... I just want them to feel like this is the most beautiful day of their lives."

"It will be," Ewan assured him, placing a friendly hand on his shoulder for a moment. "They will see in everything how hard you tried to make their day special. They will feel your love."

Wilcox looked at him. "I can't thank you enough. Not just for your help, but also for your willingness to look past my anger. It would have been so easy for you to think 'What a terrible man. I won't lift a finger to help him.'"

"Well, when I first came here, I wasn't doing it for you but for Gina. Mrs. Williams. She didn't deserve the way you treated her," Ewan said softly. "But when I saw what was happening here... I am a mountain guide and rescue worker. I just can't help rescuing, I guess." He had to smile. "Whether it is a person or a wedding party."

"You really saved the day." Wilcox looked at the flower arrangements that were filling the tables and brightening the room. "Wait a moment." He went to the flower deliveryman and asked something. The man nodded and pointed at a bucket near the platform. Wilcox went over and selected a bunch of beautiful red roses, then carried them to Ewan. "These are for Mrs. Williams. To thank her for the wonderful pies and her patience with a grumpy old man."

Ewan accepted them with the giddy feeling that Gina would be so pleased at how this had all turned out. Her reputation had been saved and Wilcox even offered an apology.

Wilcox thanked him again and said he had to make final preparations for the arrival of the happy couple and their guests. Ewan nodded, wished them a wonderful day and took his leave. As he put the red roses in the back of his car, it hit him. He was going to offer Gina a bouquet of red roses. Traditionally the flowers of love. He could only hope she wouldn't take it the wrong way. After all...

They were just friends, right?

He stood a moment staring at the roses, remembering the softness of her lips on his cheek. The kiss had felt so good. He wouldn't mind her doing that again. To thank him for saving the day.

But hey. He hadn't come out here to get anything in return. He had just wanted to help her. Like he always helped people. She needn't thank him, let alone kiss him.

He bet she had done it on impulse and was sorry already. They'd better forget about that. Both of them.

WHEN GINA SAW Ewan's car coming, she felt a wave of relief wash through her chest. He had sent her a short text to reassure her, saying that he had delivered the pies on time and Wilcox had accepted them. She had, of course, been super grateful for that knowledge, but she wanted to know the full story. How Wilcox had acted. If he had seemed really pleased with the solution. Could she still do more business with him? They would have to discuss his contracts though... She wasn't going to sign herself into new trouble. She had to look out for herself now, protect her business and her family's future.

Ewan got out and took something from the back. She strained her eyes to make out what it was. *A bouquet of flowers?*

Yes. Red roses.

Roses? For... Her heart began to beat very fast, and she glanced around as if looking for a place to hide. Could she dive into the ladies' room and not come out again for the rest of the day?

But she stood her ground and tried to breathe evenly. Maybe he had bought something at a wayside stand for Granny. Ewan was a practical, down-to-earth man. Why would he rush in with flowers for her? Red roses at that. They carried a specific meaning. He'd know that and not take the chance of being misunderstood. The center was full of people too. Mostly they didn't know the visitors, of course, but still it felt like they would have an audience.

Ewan came in through the entrance doors. He saw her and came straight to her.

Gina's heart beat even faster. She didn't know where to put her clammy hands. Her knees were like jelly and... His eyes were so warm, his smile so inviting.

He stopped in front of her and held out the roses. "For you."

Gina couldn't get a word out. She just accepted the bouquet, feeling the brush of his fingertips against hers. What was happening to her? This morning in the forest he had said she was pretty—even though she hadn't wanted to acknowledge hearing him correctly. Now he offered her red roses. And she could argue that he was so different and that their lifestyles didn't align, but her heart was telling her something else. This moment meant so much to her.

"These are from Mr. Wilcox," Ewan said, "to apologize for being so rude to you earlier on the phone. He was just frustrated that the wedding preparations weren't going as planned. But he was very happy with the new pies, and he offered these by way of reconciliation. He hopes you will accept them."

Gina was too stunned to reply. The flowers weren't from Ewan? Mr. Wilcox had given them to him to pass along? It felt like the happiness that had touched her moments ago flew away through the open doors of the center.

But why would she be so disappointed? Her sense of dejection made no sense. This was wonderful news. Wilcox didn't hate her. He didn't think her unprofessional. He apologized for what he had said. He wanted to make up. She should be jumping for joy. Her business was saved.

But all she felt was a sort of…

"Gina?" Ewan studied her closely. "Is something the matter? I thought you would be happy that Wilcox came round."

"Of course I am. It's just…such a surprise. I was certain he would still be angry. I expected bad news. Especially because you stayed away so long. Your tour left an hour ago. Grizzly took over."

"I'll thank him for that later. I, uh…got caught up in a few things to do."

"Oh." It hadn't been about her. He had been done in Yewcreek much earlier and had done other things. Fine, of course.

She looked at the bouquet for distraction. "These are lovely. I'll put them in water in the back room so they don't wilt." She turned away from him. Her heart was still pound-

ing but now with mortification. She had totally misunderstood. She had thought he was
doing this for her and that he had brought her
flowers and…

Why anyway? They were just friends. She
put the flowers in water and then pulled up
her phone to send Mr. Wilcox a thank-you
message. She wasn't about to call him as he
was probably busy with the wedding party.
But Wilcox called her a few minutes later. His
voice was urgent as he said, "My dear Mrs.
Williams, I hope you have accepted my sincere apologies by way of the roses I sent. I behaved in a terrible fashion. My nerves over the
party at my restaurant are no excuse. I should
say sorry in person, but I am tied up here for
the day."

"I understand. I'm just happy you have the
spare pies."

"Yes, your friend dropped them off. His advice about the gazebo was spot-on and his help
in getting the flowers over here was priceless.
This wedding would have been a complete di-
saster without him. You only sent him to deliver the pies, but for me he was a blessing in
disguise. Will you thank him again? I must go
now. But we will be in touch. Your apple pie
is truly remarkable."

Gina stared at her phone long after the call had ended. What had Ewan done? Helped with a gazebo? With getting flowers there? Other things to do, he had said without specifying. She had thought it was his own personal business, but he had helped out with the wedding. He hadn't wanted her to know what he had done. Typical Ewan—he was very modest and usually downplayed his involvement in things, giving other people all the credit.

But he had saved the day for Wilcox. What had he called him? A blessing in disguise.

She smiled to herself. Yes, Ewan came in to Bud's Western store to buy something and suddenly offered her a job. He delivered a few pies and then reached out and saved the whole wedding. He was like that. He saw a need and he chipped in and made everything better.

And he didn't even want anyone to know. He didn't want thanks. Because he was so modest or for another reason?

Because he is a loner, a voice in the back of her head told her. *He is the type who likes to help others, but he doesn't let people get close to him. He is always in control, knowing all the answers and helping others, but what about him? Doesn't he need people near him?*

Probably not. He had been raised without

many people around. He had chosen a remote area to live. He did tours with people, sure, but he was their guide. He wasn't part of the group. He was always on the outside and... She wondered why. Maybe he was just wired that way.

Not that it matters, she told herself. *I should be glad I found Ewan. He is a very good friend, who got me this job at the center and helped me patch things up with Wilcox. My business is still alive. I can try this more often.*

But I really need someone more reliable than Cade's buddy to deliver my pies!

CHAPTER ELEVEN

"So it was your friend who ruined everything," Lily said to Cade as they were doing the dishes that night. She slapped at him with the tea towel. "I knew men weren't cut out to care for breakable stuff like pies."

"He was in a hurry, and he only broke four," Cade countered. "I'm sure he didn't do it on purpose."

Gina leaned against the sink. "It doesn't matter because it all turned out right. Mr. Wilcox messaged me a few photos of the happy couple and the guests. The apple pies were really important to them. They met in an orchard, while apple picking. They had, uh…" She had to swallow before being able to say it. "Both lost a spouse before and believed they would never fall in love again. But then they met and discovered they could still have feelings. It's a beautiful story."

Lily cast her a worried look as if she wondered how Gina coped with this backstory to the happy couple's big day, but Cade said in a loud voice, "So all's well that ends well. I am going to have a look at the animals to make sure everything is alright for the night. Will you go with me, Gina?"

Gina pushed herself away from the sink. "Why not? I love to give Millie and Mollie some extra love before bedtime. You will read to the girls, right?" she asked Lily.

"As always. Don't worry. You can tuck them in later. It's still early enough."

Gina nodded. "Thanks for taking care of them all day. Maybe I am away too much." That was her main concern when thinking about her business and the future as a single-mom business owner. That she wouldn't have enough time and attention for her children.

Lily shook her head. "We had a lovely time, making pancakes and dressing up. You have to see the photos later. They're on my phone."

"Okay." She shouldn't worry so much. With family and friends near, it could be done.

Gina waved at her, then followed Cade outside. The evening light caressed the familiar outlines of the barns, and she inhaled the scent of Mom's geraniums. This was home to her. It felt like a warm hug. Like a comfortable bed she didn't want to get out of. But nobody could lie in bed forever.

Cade said, "So my friend was the big villain, right?"

Gina wanted to say something, but he was already continuing, "And Ewan McAllister was the golden hero."

Gina felt her cheeks flush as soon as Ewan's name was mentioned. She hated this. It was none of Cade's business anyway. Why couldn't he stop doing this? Asking her questions about what she did, how she did it…

See, you need to move away from here. Then he won't be able to butt in all the time.

"The girls can't stop talking about him either," Cade continued. *"Ewan taught us how to use a compass. Ewan taught us how to navigate."*

Gina wasn't really listening to what he said anymore. She just wished her cheeks weren't on fire. Cade shouldn't get anything into his head about Ewan and her.

"Ewan this and Ewan that," Cade pushed on. "You'd think they never saw anyone else." He glanced at her. "Just how much time are you spending with him when you're at that center?"

"Almost none," Gina said quickly. "I work in the shop with Granny. Ewan does tours and he is away with groups most of the day. He does spend time with the girls, showing them around and teaching them about the wild animals, but… It's not like he is around us much."

Cade huffed. "You wouldn't say that judging by their stories." He opened the door into the barn and let her go first. "I'm just worried they will be disappointed once he loses interest in them. I mean, to him they are just some girls who come to the center to learn about nature. He's not their friend or anything. Just a ranger."

Gina walked to Millie and brushed the donkey's soft head. "Just a ranger," she agreed. It sounded a bit half-hearted to her own mind, but that might be because she knew the truth. Ewan was much more than a ranger to her. He was…

She bit her lip. She didn't dare acknowledge it. No, she couldn't. Shouldn't. It was…wrong. Risky, dangerous.

Cade said, "I just want to protect the girls, Gina. Lily seems to think it's great that they spend so much time with this guy. She is convinced that it's good for them. But I disagree."

"But you shouldn't fight over the girls. I mean, you are so happily married. Why would you argue about something that is…"

"None of your business?" Cade supplied. He looked at her across the aisle. "It is my business, Gina. After Dad died, I became the head of our family. I take that responsibility very seriously. I want you and the kids to have a safe home here and…"

"Yes, you provided that for us, and I'm grateful you did. But I'm not staying here forever. I'm working toward my own future. My own home and life." Her baking business was giving her wings, showing her she could do things and get them right, that it was worth it to take chances.

Cade straightened up. His eyes were dark. "Did this McAllister put you up to that? To get you away from here, from us? Isolate you in a place of your own so he can play at being your friend? I don't like him and I don't trust him."

"You have never even met him." Gina felt anger rush through her veins. He was so full of prejudices. "How can you judge him that way?"

"I don't have to meet him to know he is all wrong for you."

"For me?" Gina cut across him. "You make it sound as if I'm dating him. He's just a colleague at the center. He got me the job. I like him for that. The girls like him because he knows so much about wild animals and stuff. But they also like Grizzly because he turns logs into squirrels and deer. They love Granny because she is so kind."

"They have a granny here." Cade sounded cold. "You don't need to go to strangers when you have family."

Gina blinked. What was this really about? She knew her brother well enough to try and cut through the sensible arguments he offered to the emotions that he tried to hide. "Cade, you know so many people around the district. You have friends and acquaintances. You're on committees. You are not stuck here all day with Mom and Lily because they are your family. I also need to see other people. Have conversations… It was good to meet people who didn't know about Barry and who didn't ask all the same questions. I'm tired of that."

Cade held her gaze. "Alright. So you find a job away from town and you make new friends. That's fine. Just ask yourself where it is leading to."

"Leading to?" Gina asked, on edge. "It is leading to nothing but this pointless discussion we're having. I'm working at the center, and I like the people there, and your concerns aren't going to change that."

"Okay. Fine." Cade raised his hands in the air, palms outward as if surrendering. "I just heard the girls go on about this guy and... I don't know what he is up to with my sister."

"Don't you dare go and ask him." Gina came to stand in front of Cade. "I remember what you did when I was in high school. You had seen me talking to this guy and you intimidated him, so he never dared speak to me again."

"I didn't intimidate him. I only told him to be nice to my sister."

Gina rolled her eyes. "And Clive Everett?"

"Oh no, not Clive Everett again." Cade wanted to walk away, but Gina caught his arm.

"You assumed I was dating him while we were merely working on a school project."

"I saw you together at the coffee corner."

"Yes, working on the school project." Gina exhaled impatiently. "Cade, you always jump to conclusions. Besides, I'm not sixteen anymore. I'm a grown woman with three kids. I know what I'm doing."

"Okay." Cade walked to the barn door. "Everything is fine, then. Fine with the animals to close up for the night and fine with you and the girls. It is not a problem that they are getting attached to a man who risks his life in the mountains. Who might have an accident any day."

What? How had he gotten that idea? "Ewan merely shows people around near the center," Gina protested. "He takes out families with young children and senior citizens. His job is not dangerous."

Cade stood at the door looking at her. The barn light threw shadows across his tight face. "Oh, you don't know he is also in mountain rescue? That every time tourists get lost or in trouble, they fly him out by helicopter to go and find them? That he has to risk life and limb to bring them back safely? Or do you know and think that's not dangerous either because Ewan knows what he's doing?"

Gina's knees turned to jelly, and her head was swimming. She clenched her hands to regain some calm. *Wait,* she told herself, *what?*

Her mind refused to process this bit of information. No, Ewan was a ranger, not a rescue worker. Wasn't he? He had never mentioned anything about it. Then again, he had never mentioned growing up in the desert and the jungle until this morning. There could be so much more that she didn't know about him.

Cade said, "You didn't know." He closed the

distance to her. "I can see it in your eyes. You didn't know and you do mind."

He was right, but she wasn't about to admit that. It felt like he'd moved in while she was vulnerable, undone by his revelation. What did he expect her to do? Say she'd never talk to Ewan again? "You know nothing about what I know, think or feel, Cade. You never give me a chance to share it with you. You merely assume and draw conclusions. And you treat me like a little sister that you have to protect all the time. You might mean well, I don't know, but… This shouldn't happen. Search inside yourself for the reasons why and deal with them, instead of expecting of me to change my life around for you. I know what I am doing. I have solid plans for my future, to give the children everything they deserve. Now let me go inside to the twins."

"Wait!" Cade wanted to catch her arm, but she shrank away from him and hurried to the door. She wouldn't let him see the turmoil his revelation had created. The pain she was hiding behind her self-assured words. Inside she was reeling.

What if it was true? What if Ewan was in mountain rescue?

It hurt to know he had kept something from

her. Perhaps consciously hidden the truth. After all, he now knew how Barry had died. She had told him herself during that emotional conversation. Had he then decided not to share that part of his work with her? At least not yet maybe?

Had he simply been waiting for the right moment to discuss it?

But why feel the need to keep it to himself until…

It was too late?

Because she already cared so much about him?

Because she was already…falling in love?

CHAPTER TWELVE

LILY LOOKED UP when Gina came in through the back door. "Done already?" she asked cheerfully.

Gina said, "I'll read to the girls myself. I've been neglecting them."

"No, you haven't." Lily perked her ears up at Gina's tone. "Did Cade say that to you? He can be a little insensitive sometimes, but he means well."

Gina stopped and looked at her, her eyes wide in her pale face. "He told me you argued about Ewan. Because you think he is a good friend to have for the girls and me, and Cade doesn't agree with that. But you are both bothered about nothing. Ewan is a helpful colleague and nothing more. I will always love Barry." She left the kitchen hurriedly.

Lily frowned hard. Say what? Where had that come from? Had Cade taken Gina to the barn to question her about Ewan? None too subtly, probably. That man…

Lily left the kitchen, crossed the yard with a few angry strides and went into the barn to tell Cade exactly how she felt about his tactics. He was ruining everything. Instead of letting Gina develop a bond with Ewan he was…

But as soon as her eyes were adjusted to the light, she saw Cade sitting on a hay bale, his face hidden in his hands. He looked so alone and so dejected that her heart melted, and she could do nothing but go over and throw her arms around him.

Cade stirred a moment as if he wanted to shake her off, then he pulled her into his embrace and hugged her so tightly it almost hurt. Lily said nothing but waited until he spoke first. She had made the mistake early in their marriage of trying to wring things out of him, which had never worked. She needed to let him come to her.

"I can't believe that it's actually true," Cade said in a hoarse voice. "That, that…" He seemed to search for the right word and not find it. "Supposedly friendly man actually hid from her that he is a mountain rescuer. She didn't know. I could see it in her features the moment I told her. Like…part of her died or something. She must have feelings for him. Now she knows it will never work." He raised his head and looked at Lily. His eyes were dark with hurt. "How could we have let this happen? I told you she should have taken the job with Bayliss. But you said the center was better. That she could meet new people there and make friends. Now what do you say?"

Lily stepped back from him and gave him a stern look. "I say that I don't have the faintest idea what you are talking about."

Cade sighed and then a waterfall of words poured out, sharing all his doubts and worries and how he had confronted Gina about it just now.

Lily listened with growing frustration. When he was done, she said, "Oh, Cade, how could you have done this? You sprung it on her when she wasn't expecting it. That is not the way she should have learned about it. Ewan should have told her, in his way. When he was ready."

"Oh, and what should I have done until he was ready? Kept my mouth shut until it was too late? Until she is so in love with him that she wants to go through with it even though he has a profession that will only cause her grief?" He reached for Lily's hands and squeezed them tightly. "Don't you see that he is all wrong for her? In fact, the worst man she could have possibly met and grown to like. He is a danger to her peace of mind, to the safe life she's built here with us."

"You gave her shelter for a while." Lily lowered her voice to a tender level. "But you can't keep doing that. The little bird you found fallen from the nest has grown and is now ready to try its wings. You can't keep it cooped up. You have to set it free. Even if it will be so hard to watch it go."

"But she will be hurt again. And it's not just her. What about the girls? Little Barry? Gina must think of them first."

"I'm sure she does. She is a very responsible person. She doesn't need you to make her feel guilty." Lily was still using a soft, warm tone. She knew Cade well enough to realize that behind his self-righteous defense of his actions he was just so afraid of new problems coming to his family. He had run the ranch since his dad died; a heavy load had rested on him. It had made him feel solely responsible for his family's well-being. He worried too much.

"Give Gina space, Cade, or you will only lose her. She wants to do what is right. Let her find her own path. Ewan makes her smile. Haven't you seen it? She is different the last few weeks. She hums and sings and… She's full of life again. She needs that. Barry is gone. She can't grieve for him forever." It hurt to say it out loud as Barry was Lily's brother and she had seen enough of his marriage to Gina to know they had been so happy. Accepting that Gina was moving on with her life was like feeling the loss of Barry all over. But it had to be done. For Gina's sake and the children. "She must embrace life again and opportunities."

"But not with this guy." Cade rose from the hay bale. "I have to think of a way to get her away from the center. This will only cause heartbreak, and I can't let it happen. I can't."

"You won't have to," a voice said.

Lily turned her head with a jerk to Gina, who had come in without their hearing it. Gina looked calm and collected, but that didn't say much. Lily had seen her right after Barry died, always keeping a brave face for the children. Gina was so good at that. That was exactly why she needed someone by her side, to break down her defenses and get close to her, comfort her when she needed it.

Gina said, "I didn't know, Cade. But I am glad you told me. I can only guess that no one said anything about it because they didn't want me to learn about rescue missions and…

things having to do with that, considering…" She swallowed. "It was probably meant as a kindness on their part. But it's better that I know."

Cade looked at her. His expression was full of pain. "Gina, I never meant to…"

"I know." Gina came over and gave him a hug. "I know I can rely on my big brother."

Then she turned to Lily. "And on my sister-in-law, who is also my best friend."

Lily wrapped her arms around Gina and held her tight. "We will always be there for you." She let go and looked Gina in the eye. "We will always be there for you, here on the ranch, but you also need to do things away from here. Please don't make any hasty decisions and quit at the center."

"I can't. It would be such a disappointment for Granny and the others. They need my help."

Cade opened his mouth as if he wanted to protest, but Lily sent him a scorching look that made him shut up. Gina continued, "I will keep working there, of course. And I will keep baking pies and other treats for people because that is just what I love to do. That is work. It is fulfilling. But my main focus is on my family. Raising the girls and little Barry. As best as I can, on my own. You were right, Lily. Barry isn't coming back. But I'm still here, and I will do everything I can to make my children happy." She smiled with sadness in her eyes. "I would never put them at any risk."

"We know that," Lily said and hugged her again. Everything inside her fought this development. Cade's rash action to reveal Ewan's profession, Gina's knee-jerk response—it was all wrong. Lily had so hoped that… Gina could find love again. She deserved it so much.

Gina pulled away from her. "The girls are waiting for me. Don't worry, Lily. It will be alright. You too, Cade. Don't fight over me. Be happy. Because you should be." She turned and walked away, closed the barn door softly.

Lily looked at Cade. He seemed relieved. "She took it rather well." He frowned hard as if he tried to process what he had just heard. "Maybe I was mistaken," he said hesitantly. "Maybe she never thought of this Ewan guy as a potential…" He fell silent as if he realized that what he was saying made no sense. Surely he couldn't fail to see that Gina's reaction proved she had seen Ewan as a potential partner. Otherwise, she wouldn't have been so affected by learning what he did for a living. How he was worlds away from the ideas of a safe future she had for herself and her children.

Lily said, "I don't like this at all, Cade. She says *we* should be happy. I know she's always supported our relationship. Even though she was grieving and unhappy during that summer when we met and fell for each other, she never resented us finding love."

"I don't resent her finding it, in due time. When the kids are a little older, you know." Cade gave her an honest look. "I do want her to be happy. If that is in a new relationship, why not? But it can wait a couple of years. And if it does happen, it will have to be with someone stable and…"

"Risk free?" Lily added.

"Exactly. The world is full of men who don't dangle from helicopters for a living. She just needs to meet the right one." Cade nodded and gestured to the door. "Shall we go inside for coffee? I could sure use a cup."

CHAPTER THIRTEEN

EWAN WALKED AROUND the center's garden looking for Gina. He hadn't had a chance to talk to her all day and he was almost worried she'd go home again without their having met at all. He wasn't sure what it was, but he felt nervous about seeing her. Jittery, unsure. As if handing her those roses had changed something between them. They had been Wilcox's roses. But in that split second when their fingers had touched and he had seen the look in her eyes, he had wished they were his and that he had said something to go along with the gift.

Something like, *You're so pretty*.

He had cowardly said it over the forest phone. She hadn't been able to make it out.

Or had she? Had she consciously dodged his awkward attempt at wooing her? He had so little experience with this. He was probably doing it the wrong way. She had once been swept off her feet by a suave, utterly romantic man. Of course he couldn't compare to that.

He didn't see Gina, but he did spy Stacey sitting on a log. She was poking in the ground with a stick. He came over and sat down beside her. "Hey there."

"Hi yourself." She glanced at him. "Mom isn't here. You're probably looking for her, right?"

Ewan felt his neck grow warm. How did this little girl know that?

Stacey continued, "Everyone is looking for Mom or for Ann. They always do the right things. I do the wrong things and then everyone is angry."

"What happened?" he wanted to know.

"I was playing with Ann, and I told her we could see who could jump furthest. We tried and she hurt herself. It wasn't my fault. She did it all by herself. She scraped her knee. Just a little graze, a little blood, no big deal." Stacey shrugged. "But she ran off to Mom wailing like a siren. I bet I will get a lecture now about not playing so rough."

Ewan nodded slowly. "That is understandable."

"But it wasn't my fault. It wasn't like I pushed her and she fell. She made the jump herself."

"Sure, but wasn't she pushing herself a little too hard because she wanted to compete with you? Jump further?"

"Maybe."

"So your mother might think that, uh… maybe you said something to get her to try?"

Stacey sighed. "Maybe."

Ewan stared into the distance. He had no real experience with kids beyond the settling of little squabbles between participants in his birdhouse making workshops here at the center. He wasn't a psychologist or something. What could he say to help her? He did want to help her. It was sad to see her so glum, hear her deprecating words about herself.

"People are always comparing us," Stacey said. "They say Ann is neater. Her dress is always straight and her hair brushed back. They say she is so polite and helpful. I am better at running and jumping. But no one ever sees that or cares."

Stacey's frustration was palpable. Ewan didn't know what to say. He wanted her to love herself for everything she was. But obviously, she felt like it was better to be different.

She looked up at him with her clear eyes and asked, "Which one of us do you like better? Tell me honestly. I can take it."

Ewan was taken aback by the urgency in her words. This mattered a great deal to her. What was he going to say? If he messed up now, he could lose her trust forever. But if he acknowledged he liked her better, he would not really be helping her either. Not in the heart of things.

"We are twins." Stacey's expression was sad. "We are dressed the same way. We look cute because we are each other's mirror image. People tell us that we look alike so often. But we aren't alike, you know. I want to know which one of us is better."

"Neither of you is. You're different. Ann is polite, sure, but you tell such funny jokes. And Ann remembers all the animal names I told you, but you handle the compass with skill. You can both do different things. And together you are unbeatable."

Stacey took a deep breath. "You are not going to tell me who you like better," she concluded. "But you do know it. Everyone knows who they like or don't like."

"I like both of you. You know that." Ewan felt the urge to comfort this sad, insecure little girl, but he didn't know how. What could he say to make her feel better about herself? Without having to talk down about her sister?

"Life is hard," Stacey concluded with a serious expression.

Ewan nodded agreement. "It often is. But we can decide how we want to feel about it."

"I don't understand."

"Well…" Ewan didn't want to use this example, but it was the best he could come up with. "Sometimes I have to go out and look for people. They went on a walk and got lost. Because they are from the city and they don't know the woods. Or they forget to look at the map. Or they are tired and they want to take a shortcut. Now, I know the woods very well. It's easy for me to think that they are rather stupid people."

"You should never call someone stupid, Gran says," Stacey corrected him at once.

"Right. My first impulse is to judge them and call them names for getting lost. But then I think about it, and I realize that they had reasons for what they did, or they lacked the skill to make the right decisions. I do have those skills. That puts me in a position where I can help them. I can make right what went wrong."

"That must feel great." Stacey's expression lit. "You must like that."

"I like it a lot. But it is a choice every time. I can judge people for what they do and feel superior because I know that it was wrong. Or I can decide to use my knowledge and skills to save them. That is always the better option."

Stacey looked at him with a frown as if she was trying to take it all in. "So if I know I can jump further than Ann, I shouldn't push her to try so that she loses, but I should try and help her get better at it?"

"Exactly. You have so many skills that you can teach others. The things you are good at are gifts you can share."

"That sounds great." Stacey's eyes lit, and she reached out and hugged him. "Thanks, Ewan, you are the best."

His throat constricted a moment for the faith this little girl put in him. He had doubted himself, thought he couldn't handle this, but now she let him know it was alright.

Stacey jumped to her feet. "I'm going to ask if Ann feels better. Then we can play again." She ran off, throwing her arms in the air and whooping.

She passed Gina, who came down the path. "I'll apologize to Ann, Mommy."

GINA LOOKED AFTER her daughter. She had fully expected to find a sad little girl here, or an angry one, and that it would take some persuading to get her to patch things up with Ann. But now it seemed Stacey was all ready to do so. Had she figured it out by herself? Or…

Gina's heart pounded as she spotted Ewan, who got to his feet to come over to her. She had avoided him all day long. She knew she just wanted to ask him one question. Why he had not told her about his work. But it would be an odd thing to ask. And he might wonder why it mattered so much. She supposed lots of people considered him a hero and admired him for what he did.

"I hope Ann isn't hurt badly," Ewan said as he fell into step beside her back to the center. "Stacey said it was a graze."

"Nothing serious. Ann was just angry Stacey pushed her to keep trying." Gina took a deep breath and added, "I wish she was more thoughtful and cared for Ann's feelings."

"Oh, but she does. When you first came to the center, on that Saturday you were going to meet Granny and show off your products, Stacey mentioned to me that Ann and you are afraid of avalanches."

Gina stopped and looked at him. "Avalanches?" she asked with alarm. Her heart pounded like a sledgehammer in her chest. She

VIV ROYCE 253

had to swallow before she could ask, "How did that come up in conversation?"

"We are close to mountains. The center has a…documentary about the beauty and dangers of living near mountains. It's on constant replay in our movie theater. It has a short clip of an avalanche. It wasn't shot anywhere near the center, but Stacey didn't know that. Apparently, she thought it might impact all of us here."

So she had heard right when the visitors came out of that room.

"Stacey actually saw the avalanche footage?" she asked with new panic attacking her. If anyone had asked her whether her children would ever be allowed to see shots of an avalanche, she would have said no. It would be too traumatizing since they knew their father had died in one.

"Yes. I don't know how much she saw. She sneaked in there and must have seen something because she mentioned to me that Ann and you shouldn't see it."

Oh no. Gina felt her stomach squeeze. She should never have let her daughter get hurt that way.

Ewan said, "Do you realize that? She came out and she wasn't thinking of herself or anything. No, she told me you shouldn't see it. Or Ann. She wants to protect you." He held her gaze. "She is a very sweet little girl."

"Yes and that is why I should not have brought her here. This is the wrong environment." She suddenly saw it with a breathtaking clarity. This was his world. His name even meant of the mountains. He had told her so that first day in Bud Travers's store when he had offered her the job here. She had taken his offer and made a crucial mistake going to the very world that she professed to despise. The mountains with their snow that had swept Barry away from them. Why had she not stayed away? Made sure her children would not fall in love with the great outdoors?

"Why would you think it's the wrong environment?" he asked with a frown.

"My husband *died* in the mountains." To her mind that explained everything.

But Ewan didn't seem to catch on. "Yes?" he asked, apparently waiting for more.

Gina shrugged and started walking again. He might not understand, but he hadn't been through the same traumatic experience as they had. "Mountains are dangerous. You just told me the footage at the center shows the beauty but also the dangers of this kind of terrain. Besides, you know personally because you go out all the time rescuing people." Gina didn't look at him as she said it. Anger bubbled inside her. It was so unfair. That this had to be part of his job. Of all the professions he could have had! Why had she come here, hopeful for work and forging new friendships, and why had it turned out this way? His lifestyle and priorities were just completely opposed to her own.

He seemed to wait a moment, thinking about his answer. "I know what I am doing."

"I bet Barry said the same thing when he set out with his friends that day." She clenched her hands into fists. "He was an experienced skier, and they were on an approved track. They weren't doing anything dangerous, going off trail like some thrill seekers do. They stuck to the rules, and still it went wrong. Nature is unpredictable like that."

"That's true. I can try and eliminate as much risk as I can but…"

"It's never completely safe." She took a deep breath before adding, "You could get hurt."

"I can't deny that."

"You could even die."

"I can't deny that either. But I can also die here, Gina."

"Here?" She almost jumped a foot off the

ground. "Why? What dangerous thing is out here? A bear? A mountain lion?" She looked around them as if such a predator could charge out of the brush at any moment. "You never told me that."

"I could die of a heart attack." Ewan held her gaze. "Or a stroke. I can't protect myself against death. No one can."

"That's not the same thing. You can't control that. But you can control where you go. You can stay away from dangerous places." Like she should have stayed away from this center, where her kids got confronted with their loss all over again.

"Yes, you can also stop driving a car and never take a plane."

His calm retorts infuriated her. "You're making light of it."

"No, I'm looking at the facts as they are."

Gina huffed. "I don't want facts or odds. People have told me, to my face, that skiing is really safe. That there are few accidents. Well, my husband had an accident, and he never came back from that trip. I had to explain to my children and…" She couldn't continue without bursting into tears. She tried to control her breathing to keep calm.

"I don't know how that is. And I'm not judg-

ing you. I think you did so well with them—
they're fantastic kids. Stacey is a very sensitive
little girl. She may look wild on the outside,
but she thinks things through very well. You
should be proud of her."

Gina looked at him. How did he know all of
that? Had he talked to Stacey? Had she confided in him instead of in her own mother?

*See, he is getting dangerously close to your
children. They look up to him, adore him, follow his lead. Where will that take them?* She
pushed her hands deep in her pockets. "I just
wanted you to know that… I may have made
a mistake coming to work here. I mean, I un-
derestimated how much this place would bring
back memories of things I want to forget." She
could use that as an excuse to take her leave.
Never come back here.

"You're not quitting the job, are you?" he
asked with alarm in his voice. "You can't do
that. Granny depends on your help. This is
our anniversary year. We have so many extra
activities on the calendar. And Granny adores
Barry. He is like the little grandson she never
had."

Granny, dear sweet Granny. She had no
children or grandchildren. She depended on
the people at the center to be her family. To

provide her with happy moments of love and laughter. It would be so unfair to abandon her. And maybe she didn't have to. Maybe she could find a compromise? "I don't want to quit, but... I might stop bringing the twins. I feel they are better off at home on the ranch."

"Please, Gina..." He halted her and touched her hand. "Don't do this. I realize it's hard to be here because it's bringing up memories you would have rather avoided but... You can deal with the pain. So can the girls. They have to, to make them stronger. I just told you that Stacey is very thoughtful for her age and that she cares for her sister. They can be a huge support to each other. Stacey can teach Ann to see past her doubts and insecurities and become more confident, also in her physical abilities."

"I don't know if I want that. I mean... You don't know how it is." She held his gaze. "I'm responsible for them, for their well-being. I have to make all the decisions. By myself."

"It doesn't need to be that way." Ewan stared into her eyes, with insistence. "You have friends who want to help you. Stand beside you. Support you. You are *not* alone."

Gina felt like she was sinking into the depths of those eyes, was cushioned by the warmth in his voice. *You are not alone. You are not alone.*

He didn't just say it, he had proved it. He had been there for her when she needed him, helping her to adjust here, encouraging her to expand her business. Thanks to him, she had succeeded with her pie delivery to Wilcox's restaurant. He helped her to believe in her own abilities, to become more of the woman she had been before grief had eaten away at her. He was restoring her, in every way.

Ewan leaned over. His lips came closer to hers, closer…

Gina's breathing grew shallow. She should step away, not let this happen. But she wanted it so badly. She would forever be sorry if she didn't…

His lips brushed hers with a tender touch. He took his time waiting for her to pull back if she wanted to. But she didn't. This was just right. She moved closer to him, and he deepened the kiss. She closed her eyes and fell into the security of this moment. It was like coming home. It was like…

Home? Was she at home in Ewan's arms?

But how could she be while they were so different? His way of life in a cabin in the wilderness, his loner mentality, his high-risk job. It was everything she didn't want in a man. If she had to fill out a questionnaire to describe

her ideal man, he would be living in a community, be very social, have a desk job or something totally devoid of danger. How could she
have met the exact opposite of that ideal man
and fallen for him?

She pulled back and faced him breathlessly.
"We shouldn't be doing this. This is…" She
couldn't think sensibly. She just knew it had
been wonderful to be able to feel this again,
while she had thought she never would. It was
amazing and also the worst thing, all at the
same time.

Ewan asked, "Didn't you want the kiss?"

"Yes, but that doesn't matter. We can't be together. We shouldn't. We are just too different,
there is too much dividing us. Attraction can't
change that. It only makes us…reckless." She
raised a trembling hand to her face. Touched
her lips that still ached for his tenderness.
Despite her brave words, she wanted nothing
more than to fall back into his arms and kiss
him again. "Oh, we shouldn't have done this.
Now I really have to leave."

"Gina, no, please…" Ewan wanted to reach
out for her, but she stepped back and turned
away, rushed off. Her head swam, and she
could only think of one thing to do. Get away
from the man who confused her so much.

Whose embrace had felt like the best place in the world. The man she was falling for—the last person on earth she should be with.

CHAPTER FOURTEEN

"GINA?" A HAND touched her arm and she jerked to full attention. Her mother stood beside her. There was a food smell on the air. Oh yes. She was making dinner. She had been distracted for a moment, thinking of Ewan and their kiss.

"Did something happen?" her mother asked. "You've been so quiet since you came back from the center."

Yes, something happened, Mom. The most wonderful man in the world kissed me. And I kissed him back. I think I'm falling in love with him.

And I'm so afraid.

"No, nothing happened. I'm just tired. I've been on my feet all day."

"But tonight is Nora's birthday party."

Nora was one of her best friends from town. As kids they had spent so many afternoons playing on the ranch. When Gina had moved away, they'd stayed in touch, writing letters and emails, sending Christmas cards. When Gina had come back to town, they'd met again, and it had felt like yesterday since they'd seen each other. She couldn't simply skip such a momentous occasion. But she didn't feel like going to a party either. Having to look cheerful and chatting with people all night long. She had to find some way to avoid it.

"But I have to stay home with the kids."

"Lily can look after them. She told me this afternoon she wants to do some watercolor painting. Cade is out to a meeting of the farmers' association. I'll come with you to Nora's to catch up with her parents. I haven't seen them since they moved to Canada, but I heard they're in town for the birthday party. I finally want to hear all about their new house. I saw some photos, of course, but I bet it will be much better if they can tell me in person."

Gina wanted to argue further, but Lily came in and Mom immediately asked her to babysit the children. Of course Lily agreed right away. She said with a warm smile, "You should really have some downtime, Gina. You work too hard. I can see it in your face." She came over, hugged her and kissed her on the cheek. "Have a night off. I'll finish making dinner.

You go and have a hot bath. Then after dinner you can change into something nice, do your hair... Have a fun time away from all your responsibilities."

"That's very sweet of you, Lily." Gina was glad to escape the hot kitchen and her mother's scrutiny. "I will do that." As she walked away, she glanced back and saw the look Mom and Lily exchanged. They grinned like confidantes in some secret plan. They had, of course, discussed that she worked too hard, looked pale, had to unwind, etc. It was sweet of them, and it almost brought new tears to her eyes. She was too emotional today because of everything that had happened.

She took a deep breath. There was no point in going over it again and again. It had happened. Ewan had kissed her, and she couldn't blame him for it. There had been attraction between them from the first time they'd met. He had been so kind to her, catching on to her mood and offering her the job and... He had gone out of his way to make her and the kids feel welcome. He had helped out when the delivery to Mr. Wilcox had gone awry. He had been a perfect friend. And he was becoming much more than that.

That was scary. When she had met Barry

and fallen head over heels for him, she'd been young and naive. She'd just basked in the sun of being in love. There hadn't been a single cloud in the sky. It had all been easy.

Too easy maybe. She hadn't been prepared for the pain that was to follow when her carefully constructed life had come crashing down around her ears.

Today everything was different. She was cautious, perhaps even fearful. She shied away from risks. She didn't make friends easily. And she never, ever wanted to fall in love again.

Still, it had happened. The moment she had been in Ewan's arms, had felt his lips on hers, had seemed right—like finding shelter after a storm. Ground to stand on after everything had been torn away.

But that was a lie. She was deceived by her feelings. He was handsome, yes, and kind, and good with the children. But he was also a loner, a man who needed space, who had told her that he didn't have any close friends because he had led a wandering existence from a young age. He had never had a community as she knew it here in Heartmont, and he hadn't missed it either. He was happy with the life he led, in the forest, with his dog, taking his early morning walks or sitting on the porch watching the sunset by himself.

On top of that, he had to go out there and rescue people and…do everything in his power to save lives. Probably with disregard for his own. She couldn't imagine Ewan being concerned for what might happen as long as he could do what was right. Besides, he knew he had skills; he relied on his abilities. But what guarantee was that?

She couldn't deal with such a life. Having to worry about him all the time. Trusting herself and her children to him only to find he was swept away from them too. No. They could never go through such loss again. She had to save herself from it but also, and most of all, her children. They were recovering step by step, becoming happy again, despite the heavy loss in their young lives. She couldn't put them through insecurity again. She had to make sure she offered them all the certainties she possibly could. Socially, financially.

She reached the bathroom and went in, locked the door. She stood at the basin and looked into the mirror over it. Her eyes were calm and determined. She knew what she had to do.

In fact, she had already done it. She had to stay away from Ewan. She had to avoid seeing him again. He shouldn't tell her how he felt, that he cared for her. She knew that; she had tasted it in his kiss.

He had kissed her. A wonderful man had kissed her.

She should be standing here, dancing with joy. She should feel like the luckiest woman alive because she was still able to feel after her loss. Grief hadn't numbed her or removed her need to see the tenderness in a man's eyes. It was still there and it offered hope. It breathed through her like a tender breeze, carrying the scents of spring after a long cold winter.

But she didn't feel lucky. On the contrary. She didn't want this risk in her life. No. She had to be firm and eliminate it. It was still early days. They hadn't dated or anything. They had just spent time together at the center. They had bonded over the kids, their love of nature. They had...

Whom was she kidding?

When Ewan had taken her to check on the adventure trail and he had touched her hand and whispered things to her over the forest phone, hadn't that been much like a date? Hadn't he been wooing her, trying to see what he could be to her?

Hadn't he attempted to melt her defenses bit by bit?

And he had succeeded.

If she placed her hand on her chest and felt the beating against her palm, didn't she know that he had made his way to her heart? That all her talk of being careful and not taking chances had faded when she had slowly let her guard down for him?

She took a deep breath. She had to be sensible now. This couldn't go on. Ewan had kissed her and it had been very enjoyable, but she was a grown woman, not a schoolgirl in love. She was a widow, a mother of three. She had the future to think of. She had to keep this man away from her family. He meant well, and he was a nice person, but his lifestyle and profession were just out of the question. If she had known earlier...

Yes, if she had only known earlier and been able to somehow prevent things from taking this turn...

She shook her head abruptly and turned the tap to fill the bath. She had to relax, dress up, be cheerful tonight. She could think about the rest tomorrow.

EWAN SAT ON the bench in front of his cabin and stared at the trees surrounding him. Normally he found this a very calming view. But tonight his head was in such turmoil that he felt almost like the trees were oppressive, closing in on him. He wanted to leave and run, forget about all the thoughts going through his head. He wanted to get tired, too tired to think and second-guess his actions. He shouldn't have kissed Gina. But if he shouldn't have, then why had it felt so good? Not just for him, for her too. She had answered the kiss. He was sure.

Not that it seemed to matter. She had said they shouldn't have, that she was leaving…

He had to talk her out of that. But how? He could never convince her that his work wasn't dangerous. She was dead set on assuming that it was. He couldn't blame her considering what she had been through.

How was it possible that he had fallen in love with a woman whose husband had died in a skiing accident? Someone who hated mountains and snow and winter sports and…rescue work…

He exhaled in a huff. It was much more than that. He could chalk it all up to his profession, but he knew deep down that Gina's reservations were connected to much more than that. Their personalities, for starters. She was much more outgoing and social than he was. An easy talker. Someone who liked to be around others, while he loved to be alone. Needed to be alone. After too much time with groups, he had to turn his back on the civilized world and wander through the wilderness to reconnect with the forces of nature.

He lived a simple life without luxury. His cabin had electricity from a generator; he cooked on a woodstove. He had very little in terms of possessions. Gina would probably want more for her family. His salary offered possibilities, maybe, but it would also mean giving up on the freedom he had out here.

He would need to commit not just to her but also to her children. He had so little experience dealing with kids on a deeper level. Sure, Stacey had listened to him and even thanked him for his advice, but it wouldn't always be like that. She might also someday say she hated him and run away from him, and what would he do then? Could he be a father figure to those lonely children? Him, the mountain man with the lack of social skills...

A beeping sound made him jump upright. It was his pager, calling him out on a mission. As soon as he heard that familiar sound, he followed a set routine. Go inside, open the cupboard where his backpack was with all he needed. Swing it onto his back, check everything in the cabin was turned off, pick up Fuzzy… She knew the drill and was circling him, her tail wagging. To her, the beeps didn't mean a mission with lives at stake, but treats at the heli center where he left her in the good care of the emergency operator.

"Come on, girl," he said to her as they went inside to get ready. "I'm almost glad that I don't have to sit here all night pondering. That I can do something. Even if it is the very thing Gina doesn't want me to do."

ONCE THEY WERE up in the air, Ewan's focus was laser sharp. He sat in the back of the chopper, watching the landscape flash by below. He had a general idea of the area where he would be dropped and of the direction he had to take to find the missing people. It was an elderly couple this time. They had set out on foot to take a hiking path that led from the center to a trail cabin halfway up a mountain. Once they reached the cabin, they were supposed to call in via the radio. They hadn't called, so it was assumed that they hadn't made it. Cell phone reception in this area was sketchy at best. They may not be able to call for help if they needed it.

He had to go and find them. He hoped they had stayed on the path. That would be easy to follow even as darkness set in. He had a good headlight and additional lighting to work with. But in his experience, people often did weird things when they panicked. If one of them had taken a fall and hurt themselves, the other might have left the path to follow an assumed shortcut to get help. And then it would be very difficult to locate them as night fell.

But he wasn't looking too far ahead yet. He was focusing on the first step. The chopper would drop him in a clearing near the cabin. He would check that first to make sure they weren't there. Maybe they had forgotten to radio in, or the radio hadn't been working. It could be as simple as that. Once he had made sure they had not arrived, he could take the next step and follow the path back to the center to see if he could find them along the way.

As he watched the trees below, he saw birds take flight as the chopper passed overhead. This time was just like many, many others before. And still it was different. Because he felt different. Tonight, for the first time in his career as a rescue worker, he was aware that he was taking a risk and that he might not come back from this mission—and that it would be a shame because he had so much to come back to.

He had always been very clinical about the dangers. Yes, there were risks, but he was a professional, and it would all be alright somehow. Now he sensed a sort of tremor in his chest. He heard Stacey say, "You are the best," and he felt her arms around his neck. He saw Gina's smile, the beauty of her face when she was absorbed in work or played with her son. He had so much to go back to, so much to lose if this went wrong.

He could suddenly understand her fear. If you loved someone, then the idea of anything happening to take that love away again was terrible.

It convinced him all the more that he did love her. That this wasn't a passing feeling, an interest in a beautiful woman with a tragic past. No. This was so much more. It had forced him to do things he would otherwise never have done and to discover he could do more than he had figured. Maybe even that he was more socially adept than he had thought? Perhaps it was even an advantage to be less of a talker—he gave Stacey space to speak her mind without telling her a thousand things right off the bat. He cared for her and honestly wanted to be there for her and Ann and Barry. Maybe he could be a positive father figure to them… If he was willing to take the chance.

He'd have to take a leap into the unknown like he did when the chopper dropped him off. He had an idea of what he was up against, but reality was always different. Still, he had never said no to a mission. And he wasn't about to say no now. He and Gina had to do something with this chance. Not let it pass due to worry and distrust.

They deserved a chance. Ewan and Gina. Gina and Ewan. It had a nice ring to it.

He smiled to himself as the chopper made the descent to the drop-off location. He would tell her as soon as this mission was over. That she had to give them a chance. Because they deserved it. They were worth it. And together they could overcome anything in their path.

LILY BRUSHED THE hair away from Barry's face. He was so cute when he was sleeping. She couldn't tear herself away from his cot but stood watching him as he lay there so peacefully, his little fist clutched to his cheek. It hadn't been a chore at all to stay at home with the children. She loved them so much. It wouldn't always be like this. She knew that. Gina would someday have her own life again. She had to have her own life again. Cade didn't think so. He wanted to keep her here forever. Protect her against any harm. Make her safe. He meant well, but... It wasn't right. Gina should have a chance to stand on her own two feet with the children. Even if it hurt to let them go.

She heard a car engine outside and left the bedroom quietly to go see who it was. It was a little early for Cade to be back from his meeting. And knowing Mom she'd try to keep Gina at the birthday party as long as possible, to give her a chance to unwind away from her obligations at home. Who would call at this hour?

She opened the back door and went into the yard. An unfamiliar SUV sat there, and a man got out. He wore a jacket that had a tear on the shoulder and there was a bloody graze on his cheek. He came straight at her and asked breathlessly, "Is Gina Williams in?"

"No, she went out to a birthday party. Can I help? I'm Lily Williams, her sister-in-law."

"Oh, Cade's wife," the man said. He extended a hand. "Ewan McAllister."

"Oh, yes, you got Gina the job at the tourist information center. Do come inside. Do you want something to drink? Coffee? Or homemade lemonade? You look, uh…like you have been hiking."

"I've been on a rescue mission."

"Rescue mission?" Lily's eyes grew wide. "Oh, I hope no one was seriously hurt."

"No, no. An elderly couple had gone missing. They were supposed to arrive at a trail cabin, but they never called in. I was dropped by chopper to make sure they were okay. It turned out that they had never gotten beyond the halfway point. The woman had slipped and strained her ankle. Her husband tried to half carry her to the cabin. He figured it wasn't far, but it was a lot further than he thought. When I found them, they were both exhausted and glad to accept help. I carried her to the cabin and looked at her ankle. It wasn't anything serious, so they decided to stay there for a few days. The cabin is pretty basic, but it has all you need to enjoy a peaceful stay in the wilderness. And via the radio they can always call in if they need anything. I'll probably go and look in on them in a day or two. Just to make sure they're alright."

"I see. Well, come on in." Lily went ahead of him. "I had expected something more, uh… dramatic considering your appearance."

"My appearance?" Once inside, Ewan

checked his clothes and found the tear on his shoulder. "A nail stuck out of the cabin doorpost and my sleeve got caught while I carried the woman inside. It's too bad because this is my best outdoor jacket."

"I can try and mend it," Lily offered.

"No, no, I can do that myself."

"Okay. Won't you sit down?" She gestured at the leather club chair by the fireplace. "Coffee or lemonade?"

"Lemonade. I have enough adrenaline going around to sit up all night, so no coffee please."

"Okay." Lily picked up the pitcher and poured two glasses of her mother-in-law's lemonade. "There you go. Do you also want a wet cloth for the graze on your cheek?"

GRAZE ON HIS CHEEK?

"No, thanks, I'll look after that later." Ewan felt like he had come calling to the home of the girl he adored looking like a scruffy stray. But he wasn't here to make a good impression.

Or... Whom was he kidding? Of course he wanted to make a good impression. But most of all he wanted to talk to Gina and tell her how much she meant to him. Whether she wanted to keep working at the center or not. But... They had to see each other again. They had to give their relationship a chance. He was willing to work hard for her, turn his loner life-style around.

Lily sat down opposite him in a rocking chair. It creaked as she settled into a rhythm, back and forth. "It's too bad Gina isn't here," she said. "But Nora is her best friend from childhood. They became close again after Gina returned."

"I see." Ewan felt the cold of the lemon-ade through the glass against his fingertips. He wasn't sure how to kill time until Gina came. And when she did come, how he'd get her alone. It had probably not been a very good idea to come here. He should have thought it through better. But his logical reasoning seemed off tonight.

Lily said, "So how are things at the center?"

"Good." He took a sip of lemonade. "This is nice—not too sweet, not too sour."

"My mother-in-law won prizes with it, at the local fair." Lily twisted her wedding band.

"Always nice to have a family recipe. My mother used to make caramel candy for me. It was about the only sweet treat I ever got. We didn't have much living in the wilderness like we did. But that candy was easy to make, and it didn't go bad in the moist heat of the tropical rainforest." As he told her more about his childhood, he realized that earlier when he'd shared with strangers, he'd felt a need to make them see that it had been a good childhood and that his parents hadn't done him any harm by raising him the way they had. But now as he sat here by the friendly crackling fire with the cool drink in his hand, he just felt at ease with himself and the past, with the choices he had made for his life and how those had taken him to where he was today. He had always been able to adjust to a new place and new challenges, and he would also find his way into the new territory of having a relationship and raising children. A car engine resounded outside. His heart skipped a beat, and he clenched the glass. Was it Gina?

Lily stood and rushed to the window. "My husband is home from his meeting. I'll go and say hi." She disappeared outside.

Ewan couldn't resist standing up to see if he could spy anything from the kitchen window. Because he was rather tall, he could just catch a glimpse of a car parking and then a figure stepping out. Lily met the new arrival, and they talked for a few moments. He guessed that maybe they were so much in love that they rushed to fall into each other's arms as soon as one of them had been away, but he had a strong impression she had gone out to tell her husband that he was in here. Why would she though? If he was merely a colleague of Gina's…

Lily came back in gesturing busily at the man following her. "This is my husband, Cade. Cade, this is Ewan McAllister."

"Good evening." Cade shook his hand. "It's a little late for a social call. Is anything the matter?"

"No, not at all. I was just, uh…in the neighborhood, and I wanted to ask Gina a question about the anniversary celebrations. The tourist center was opened seventy-five years ago so there will be festivities all through the summer. They will be kicked off in two weeks' time, on Saturday with a big event. Barbecue, that sort of thing."

"I see." Cade's expression was doubtful. He probably wondered why a question couldn't be asked over the phone.

"I would like to show you the barn," Cade said. His wife immediately shot him a suspicious look. But Cade gestured to the back door, and Ewan could hardly refuse to come along. He put his glass away. "Maybe I had better come back some other time," he tried.

"Or call Gina. I mean, it's obviously not a good moment now."

"No, it's fine," Cade said. "I want to show you around. This ranch has been family owned for generations. We're very proud of it."

Having just shared tales of his own childhood and the way in which his folks had raised him, how could he refuse?

Outside Cade gestured to the barn and Ewan followed. It was a beautiful quiet night with a host of stars in the sky. He wished Gina had come home, and he could have looked at the stars with her. They would have talked or just said nothing. Their story had unfolded page after page, and they had to have confidence that it would keep doing so. If they let it.

Cade opened the door and turned on the lights. Immediately a donkey started to hee-haw. "That is one of the donkeys Gina brought along when she came to live here," Cade explained. "That one is called Millie, the other Mollie." He brushed the donkey's nose. "The girls love them."

"I can imagine. They look very sweet."

"They also have guinea pigs here. And they are raising a kid goat that was abandoned by its mother." Cade looked around him. "They really love animals."

"I noticed. They are eager to learn anything they can about animals. Also the animals that live in the Rockies."

"I know. Stacey showed me pictures of elk and bears. She talked about you nonstop." Cade looked straight at Ewan.

Ewan didn't know what to say. He almost felt like he should apologize, but he wasn't even sure what for.

"I hate to admit this," Cade said softly, "and I have never said it to Gina, but going to that center of yours has done the girls a world of good. Stacey has become more responsible toward Ann, and Ann isn't so caught up in her own little world anymore. I have spent so much time with them since they lost their father that I've come to know all their little ways. I can tell their mood by just looking at their faces."

Ewan studied the emotion in the other man's features. Here was someone who cared intensely for the fatherless little girls that had come to live with him.

Cade said, "It was so heartbreaking to see their sadness when they first came to us. I wanted to comfort them and make it all better, but I didn't know how. Maybe it wasn't even possible. They had lost their daddy, and no one could change that. But over time they could find some joy in life again and… Going to the center has been a big step. I see the happiness in them, and I'm glad that it's back. That is as it should be." Cade eyed him honestly. "I just want you to know that I'm very grateful that you have done this for them. We couldn't achieve that. Maybe we were too close to them…"

"And to the loss." Ewan said it softly. "They lost their father, but you also lost a brother-in-law. Someone who was part of your family."

Cade looked away. An expression of pain crossed his features. Ewan continued, "I know how hard it is as a man to acknowledge how you feel. Somehow you always have to be the one who knows all the answers. The others need you. So that is the part you play. And you play it well. I'm sure that the girls have benefited a lot from all you did for them."

Cade nodded slowly. "I hope so. I hope I have made life easier for them. Even if I couldn't make them happy again. I guess I felt for a long time like nothing would ever make them happy again." He stared at the floorboards.

Ewan waited for him to go on. To say things he might not be able to say to Gina, their mother or even his wife. Because a man didn't make himself vulnerable so easily.

Cade continued softly, "Lately I have seen that they are happy again. That there is life back in their faces, in their eyes. They can really look ahead to a future and… It is so good to realize that is happening."

"But?" Ewan asked in a low voice. "There is a *but*, isn't there?"

"Yes. I'm also afraid for them. That the hurt will come back in their lives. It shouldn't. You know."

"I know." Ewan said it and with it came the realization that maybe, just maybe he wasn't the one who had made it all better but who had made it all worse. Because the joy that had come back into their lives was threatened by him. By the feelings he had evoked in Gina. She was attracted to him, maybe, or she felt tender because he had helped her, but she didn't want to feel that. It was a risk she had to avoid. For her own sake and for her little family.

Didn't he understand? Didn't he care for her, the girls, Barry? Didn't he want them to be happy…even at his own expense? He could try to convince himself that the differences between them were hurdles they could overcome. That they were challenges that could be conquered. But Gina wasn't looking for challenges. She deserved to have it easy for a while. To focus on her baking business and her family, on building a happy home for them.

If Cade had gone against him and had accused him of being a threat to Gina, he would have argued with him trying to prove the opposite. But now that the man had made himself vulnerable, sharing his deepest fears, he couldn't respond with anything but understanding. After all, they had something in common: their desire to protect Gina and the little ones.

"I know what you mean," he said to Cade. "And I can assure you that there won't be any hurt coming to their lives at the center. It will always be a safe place for them to explore and make friends. Friends who will always do what is right for them."

Cade nodded. Something of relief flashed across his features. He reached out his hand to Ewan. "It's great that we understand each other. Have a common goal. Nice to meet you."

Ewan took the outreached hand and squeezed it. "Nice to meet you too."

His mission here seemed accomplished in a different way than he had intended. He had wanted to convince Gina to give them, their relationship, a try, but he wasn't so sure anymore that it was the best thing for her. Maybe he should just be a reliable colleague to her and a good friend. Cade had just said how the center had made Gina and the kids happier. And that was what counted—to protect their newfound joy for life.

CHAPTER FIFTEEN

GINA LET THE girls out of the back of the car. "Now, you stay together all of the time. I don't want you to go wandering off. There will be a lot of people around today. You understand?"

"Sure, Mommy." Stacey smiled up at her, then pulled her sister along. "We're going to look for Ewan."

Ewan. Gina almost flinched at the name. She had managed to keep the girls away from the center with excuses for the past two weeks, but now it was the day of the big anniversary celebrations kickoff, and she couldn't have denied them that. They had been so excited about it, counting the days until it was finally time for the big event, the party games and the barbecue.

She looked across the roof of the car at her mother, who had extracted Barry from his car seat and lifted him in her arms. She'd offered to drive them out here and take care of Barry during the day so Gina would have her hands free to chat to people and partake in activities. Gina felt like she needed Barry as a shield or at least an excuse to rush off when things became uncomfortable. But her mother's offer had been so kind, and it would have looked very odd to refuse.

She took a deep breath. Her heartbeat fluttered like she was a teenager going to a school dance. Would the handsome guy she had admired from afar even notice her nice dress?

She glanced down at the red dress with yellow flowers. It was simple, but this was a day event, and she didn't want to look overdressed. She didn't want to look as if...she was trying to get his attention?

They had talked over the phone, had exchanged messages to get things organized for the event today. Also, after the successful wedding at Mr. Wilcox's restaurant she had received more orders for larger numbers of pies and had been busy baking. Despite her full schedule, she had been here at the center three times to help Granny in the gift shop, but she hadn't seen Ewan at all then. He had been busy with tours and... It was like he was avoiding her. Was he sorry he had kissed her?

A stab of regret pierced her at the idea. No,

he shouldn't be sorry. He should…want to kiss her again? But why, if they could never be together anyway?

Grow up, she told herself sternly. *He kissed you; you kissed him back. Then you both woke up and realized it just isn't smart to start a relationship. You are too different, and you can't risk involving the children in a relationship that might end after a few weeks or months. You have to be certain or not try at all. So now he is avoiding you to make sure it isn't painful on both ends. That is very gentlemanlike.*

But why did he come to the ranch?

Lily had told her Ewan had been there, on the night he had kissed her. That he had come from a rescue mission and had looked worn. Her heart had gone out to him, and at the same time the words *rescue mission* had filled her with fear. She could never live that way. It was better they were just friends.

She followed her mother, who carried Barry in her arms. The parking lot was almost full, and the sound of voices filled the air. There were people everywhere, checking out the garden, the center or going out in groups for a tour. There were extra volunteers today to make sure everything went smoothly.

Gina carried two big shopping bags full of

boxes filled with apple pies for the coffee corner. She had more bags with buns and cakes in the back of the car.

"Can I lend a hand?"

At the sound of his voice, her heart skipped a beat. She didn't dare look up at him. "Sure." She held out her arm in his direction and he took the shopping bag from her hand, his fingertips brushing her skin. Her stomach squeezed, and she wished she could get him away from all these people and kiss him again. She wanted to find out if that feeling had been real or just a dream, a fleeting illusion. When Barry had died, she had believed she would never love again. It seemed a miracle that she could have these feelings. But if it was a miracle, a wondrous thing in her life, why was she so keen to avoid it? Was she throwing away her chance at happiness?

"The other one too?" Ewan asked.

"Yes, please, then I can get the buns from the car." Gina held out the second shopping bag to him. She still avoided looking him in the eye. She was nervous about what she might see there. Would it be just neutral friendliness...or a warmer feeling that confused her and upset her carefully organized world?

"I'll take them inside to Granny," Ewan said

and walked away. Now she did dare lift her eyes and look after him. His back was straight as always. He wore a dark blue shirt and jeans. His aftershave still lingered in the air.

She had to pull herself together to go and get the other things from the car. Carrying them inside, she spotted Ewan coming back out of the coffee corner, where he had apparently already delivered the pies. Their gazes met and she almost stopped in her tracks. He looked at her across the room, and it was as if the world stopped turning, As if there were no people there but the two of them and she was pulled to him by an invisible cord. She walked over, her knees filled with jelly. Ewan reached for the bag in her left hand. "You must have been baking for days to make all this. I heard you also had orders for your business around town. Isn't it all becoming a bit much?"

"No, I like to be busy. It wasn't any trouble." She glanced at him as he walked beside her. His face was even more suntanned than she remembered. He had to have been outdoors a lot. To keep out of her way?

Lily had told her that Cade had shown Ewan around the ranch. It had struck Gina as a little odd that Cade had offered to do so. After all, he barely knew Ewan and had earlier shown no sign of any personal interest in him. Ewan wasn't a rancher, so Cade hadn't shown him around to share their mutual interests in farm life. Had he used the tour to tell Ewan to stay away from her? If he had, how had Ewan taken that?

An uncomfortable feeling wriggled in her stomach as she looked at Ewan's tense features. "Have you been busy preparing for today? You look, uh…a bit tired."

Now he had to smile. "Thanks, I guess."

"It's not meant as a criticism," she rushed to say. "I just… Well, we haven't seen much of each other these past two weeks."

"I thought you wanted that." Ewan stopped and looked her in the eye. "Didn't you want that?"

The eagerness in his tone and eyes took her by surprise. As if it mattered so much to him that she would deny she wanted distance.

But she did want distance. Didn't she? Confused, she said, "It seemed better."

The enthusiasm in Ewan's expression faded, and he said in a flat voice, "Yes, of course. It must be better." It sounded as if he had tried to convince himself of that and had failed.

Gina felt a stab of pain in her chest. How could she be so heartless? Ewan had been so good to her and the girls. He had become a friend.

"Look…" She put her hand on his arm.

He held her gaze. Again there was that flash of hope as if he was just waiting for a signal on her part that it was okay.

"I, uh…just want us to act normal around each other, you know. Otherwise it would be painful."

He nodded. "I totally understand. And I agree." He turned away to take her things to Granny.

Somehow this practical approach wasn't very satisfying either. She felt like a heel for treating him this way. He was obviously still interested in her. And she couldn't deny what she felt the moment they were face-to-face.

But she couldn't give him false hope either. Given all the complicating factors, the responsibility she bore for her family, she wasn't getting together with him.

Ever.

I AGREE, he had said. And he did agree that they had to act normally around each other, or other people would notice and get ideas. He didn't want people to speculate about Gina and him. It would harm her reputation, and he didn't want her to feel embarrassed. She had come to work here, in a safe environment, and he shouldn't ruin it for her.

Still, something inside him didn't agree with this setup at all.

He was in love, totally, completely in love, maybe even for the first time in his life, and now he shouldn't act on it?

He shouldn't tell the woman he had fallen for that he cared for her, enough to be willing to give up his solitary lifestyle and become part of her family? He wasn't sure exactly how he would make it all work, but he wanted to try. Because she and the children had become so important to him. More important than his freedom, his work, anything else in his life.

In the past the idea of commitment might have felt like a sacrifice on his part. But now he knew he would be privileged if she allowed him into her family circle. If he got the chance to be her man and a father figure for the kids. He would never be their actual father, and that was alright. They had a father, who had left them prematurely, who would always have a place in their hearts. He wasn't competing with Barry. He just wanted a chance to offer whatever support he could. A shoulder to lean on, a listening ear, a helping hand. He might not always have all the answers, but he could at least be there for them like he had been there for Stacey when she wanted to talk. That time, he had noticed that he could do the social thing even without knowing how. It was a matter of tuning in to his own feelings and responding instinctively to what she needed. He could do it if he just allowed himself to feel instead of always rationalizing everything. He wanted to be a part of what they were: a family who stood together, who laughed and cried together. He no longer wanted to be on the outside looking in on what others had. He wanted to be a part of it, shape it together with Gina. Take responsibility for it too.

But she didn't trust him. Or maybe she didn't trust feelings? If she didn't, he could understand. He had always thought that being rational about things was far better. It could help you keep your life on track. In the wilderness it could even mean the difference between getting out alive and dying. If you panicked, if you lost your cool, it could be the last mistake you ever made.

But today he realized that he had thrown all kinds of feelings onto a giant heap and condemned them as impractical and even unnecessary. He had forgotten that it was good to feel. That even now as he stood here, aware of how uncomfortable this all was, he wasn't sorry for what he felt or that he had started to feel it. It seemed right. Gina was worth all his tenderness and affection. She deserved to be loved and cared for. As did her girls and that little boy.

"I just sold that big eagle sculpture," Grizzly's voice boomed beside him. "You know, the one down the adventure trail? Someone saw it and fell in love with it. I normally never agree to sever the sculpture and take it away from the forest where it belongs, but he offered such an outrageous sum I decided to make an exception. This is very good for the center. We do need to do some repairs this summer season and add some extra informational plaques and stuff for kids."

"I'm glad to hear it," Ewan said. His distracted tone provoked a raised eyebrow on Grizzly's part. The older man studied him. "Not in the mood today? That is strange. You worked so hard to make this day special."

"I have a lot on my mind. Rescue work..." Ewan gestured vaguely. He hoped Grizzly would take that as an explanation and not ask any more questions.

Grizzly nodded with a grunt. "You are always rescuing people, Ewan. That's a good thing. Commendable. But you should also let them rescue you. I mean, from being alone all the time. Today is a day for socializing. Don't stand here and think about being elsewhere. Enjoy the here and now. Go and play with those kids. Or take a coffee out to your lady."

"My lady?" Ewan repeated with a sheepish look.

Grizzly grinned. "I may not be the most astute reader of human behavior, but it's obvious that you and Gina make a great pair."

"I wish you wouldn't say that out loud. I'm sure she doesn't see me that way. It would be painful if there were rumors. She might not want to work here anymore."

"And that would be terrible." Grizzly nodded sagely. "I see you've got it bad. You can't bear the idea of not seeing her again."

Although that was the truth, Ewan didn't want to admit to anything even close. "Look, please don't say any of this to me or her or anybody else. It's just…not done. You get it?"

Grizzly shrugged. "Oh well, if you feel that strongly about it. But I am telling you she likes you. I saw her look at you just now and…"

"You must be mistaken. She doesn't feel

anything special for me." Or rather, she doesn't *want* to feel anything special for me.

"If you say so…" Grizzly rubbed his huge hands and looked at the center. "I'll go inside to tell Granny I sold the statue. I think I also earned an extra slice of apple pie." He walked away humming.

Normally Ewan would have called after him to inquire how many slices of apple pie he had already had. But now he was too stunned to do so. How had Grizzly concluded that Gina cared for him? What had he seen in her expression?

Nonsense, he tried to calm his pounding heart. *It's just wishful thinking on Grizzly's part. He wants her to like me, and then he thinks he sees it in her eyes.*

But why would Grizzly even want such a thing? He wasn't a matchmaker, like Granny. He was a giant of a man who lived for his wood carving and his outdoor adventures. He was a little rough around the edges and, like he had admitted himself, not exactly a close student of human behavior. How come he had caught on to the tension between Gina and him? The attraction, the tenderness.

And he had also said Ewan needed someone to rescue him. Wasn't that a way to put into words what he himself had started to discover? That feelings weren't always bad and it could pay off to open up and become part of a bigger whole?

Ewan frowned hard. Maybe Grizzly's prod was meant to strengthen his own intentions? To pursue Gina regardless of her wishes to be left alone? After all, she had kissed him back, so he knew it wasn't for a lack of feeling that she had rejected him. It was something else. Fear maybe? Uncertainty of whether she was allowed to love again after her husband had died?

Whatever it was, he had to show her that he was there for her. That he kept on loving her even if she said she couldn't love him back.

Because she was the one for him. The one who might be his polar opposite character-wise but who completed him. For her, he'd leave his beloved cabin and move to a place more suited for a young family. He could still sometimes go into the forest and watch the animals and be alone, but his home would be no longer in the woods but with her and the children.

And it didn't matter how hard it would be to convince her that they deserved a chance to be together.

However hard it was, it would be worth the effort.

GINA HANDED OUT a few more plates with slices of apple pie and then stood back with a sigh. She raised a hand to quickly sweep a strand of hair back from her face. It was hot inside with all of those people.

Granny smiled at her. "We've almost sold out. I heard so many people say how delicious your pie is. I'm sure you will get more baking assignments from this event."

"I hope so. After the wedding in Yewcreek, things took off, but you never know. If the interest winds down again..." She felt the weight of responsibility like a stone on her chest. Could she make it work in the long run? Wouldn't she mess up and let down the people who had supported her so far? Her mother, Cade and Lily...

Granny put a hand on her arm. "You are doing a wonderful job, Gina. With your baking business, but also with your children. You have to do so much on your own, but you are strong enough to do it and do it with a smile." She squeezed her arm. "Remember how I told you about my husband? And how he died and I was left all alone and I always stayed on my own, because I still loved him?"

Gina nodded. Her throat constricted at the idea of such enduring love. At the same time, it seemed very hard to be alone all your life. She ached for companionship, for someone to share the load.

Granny said, "I wasn't totally honest with you. I did fall in love again. He also loved me. He asked me to marry him." She swallowed. Her eyes were sad in her pale expression. "I said no. I turned him down because I was too afraid to try. I was worried it wouldn't be like my earlier marriage had been or that I couldn't have faith that it would last. That I would be hurt again and have to deal with new pain and grief. I gave myself a million reasons why it wouldn't work, and for a long time I believed in those. But as I grow old now, alone, I know that… I made a mistake. I should have accepted his offer. Because love is a really special thing. You shouldn't reject it when it comes your way."

Gina stared at Granny. Why was she suddenly telling her this story? It seemed almost like advice…advice that fit her situation perfectly. Love had come her way because Ewan had.

He didn't say he loves you, she told herself sternly. *He kissed you. So he feels attracted to you. That may well be, but it's not a base for commitment. Ewan is a loner. He read-*

ily agreed that it was better not to talk about what happened and just act normal. Maybe he is even sorry he kissed you.

Granny said, "Life can be hard to figure out, Gina. Sometimes you are sure you have to act and you do, and later you regret it and wish you hadn't been so eager. But more often you shy away from things because you are too cautious, and you miss out on the good things that could have been."

"I have good things," Gina said hurriedly. "I have my family—the twins and Barry. I love them so much. They mean everything to me, and I will do anything to provide for them and keep them safe."

"I know that. But I wonder if you are disregarding your own happiness in the process. You seem to think you have to focus fully on them and you can't have a relationship but…"

"Who says I even want a relationship?" Gina asked. She clenched her hands nervously. "I'm perfectly happy the way I am now."

As she said it, she caught sight of Ewan passing through the crowd. He seemed headed in their direction. Her heart began to beat fast. "I, uh…better go and check if there isn't any more apple pie in the back of my car." She knew there wasn't, but she wanted to get away from here. There was a side door. She could avoid Ewan. She should. If she looked into his honest eyes and remembered how good it had felt to be in his arms, she might… Go back on her decision?

She walked through the side door and went into the garden. It was buzzing with people. She looked left for a moment wondering if a little walk would do her good. It was warm in the sun, but there was also a pleasant breeze that brought some relief to her hot cheeks. She walked down the path trying to slow down and not rush as if something was chasing her. Was it her guilty conscience? She might tell Granny she didn't need love, but her heart was saying something else.

Despite her belief that she'd never feel anything like love again, there was this tender feeling inside her, only just awakening. She wanted to blossom again, like the apple trees in the ranch's orchards at the end of a long winter—to feel light again, so light she was almost weightless. She wanted to run downhill with her arms spread wide, laughing all the way. And there had to be someone waiting to catch her and swing her up in the air and put her down again and kiss her.

Not just someone, but Ewan. Dear kind-hearted Ewan, who had shown her how to take steps and believe in herself. Ewan, who had changed her life around, who…

She heard Stacey's voice high above the chatter of other children. "This is a compass, and it always points to the north. When you are lost, you can use it to find your way. In the forest you can get lost and then when night falls, it is dangerous. So it is important to be able to find your way back home."

Dangerous. Did she say *dangerous*? Why was her little girl talking about something dangerous?

How did she know what a compass was? And how to use it?

Gina walked into the leafy canopy of the little hut that had been built in the garden. She looked at the group of five—three girls and two boys—who sat on the ground cross-legged listening to Stacey. She held out her hand with something resting on it. A compass. She explained with a serious expression what she saw and how the needle moved as she turned the compass in her palm.

Gina stood motionless watching her daughter. Stacey was usually just playing games and getting into scrapes and here she was teaching other kids something important. A life skill.

But that wasn't what Gina wanted at all. Her little girl shouldn't know about the dangers of the forest, about getting lost. She didn't need a compass to get back home because she had her mother to rely on. She was only seven. She should be taken by the hand and guided.

"Stacey…" Gina tried to keep the annoyance out of her voice. "Come inside with me for apple pie."

The other kids looked at each other and their expressions said, oh yummy, apple pie.

Stacey said, "Let me finish this, Mommy. Ewan said it was important to teach others what you know. To help them."

"It is. But you are finished now. Run along, children." She gestured at the children to go. They rose to their feet, brushed down their clothes and ran off.

Ann remained seated on the ground. "I thought it was fun, Mommy," she said in defense of her sister.

Gina took a deep breath. "How did you learn about the compass?"

"Ewan taught us," Ann said quickly. "He also told us to carry an alarm whistle." She pulled it from her pocket.

"He told us you can't drink creek water because you might get sick. But you can cook it or use a filter to make it clean," Stacey supplied. "And he taught us to tell time by looking at the sun in the sky. It is way cool."

"I bet it is." Gina's stomach was filled with ice. "But why would you need to know all that?"

"For when we go hiking or camping." Stacey looked all excited. "There is a summer camp up in the mountains. Ewan said he'd ask you sometime if we could go."

"I'm not sure I want to go," Ann said. "I don't like sleeping away from home."

Gina reached out a hand to her. "Don't worry, darling, Mommy doesn't want you to go to summer camp."

Ann scrambled to her feet and put her hand in Gina's. Looking up at her, she said, "But maybe it would be fun to go camping with Ewan if all of us went. If you came along too."

Hiking, camping, being outdoors, in the mountains… Kids needed skills for that, apparently. They needed to know about water that could make them sick and how to find their way if they got lost and… Ewan had such different views of raising children. He wanted them to take risks and try things on their own. How could they ever be together if they didn't see eye to eye about something as important as the children's upbringing?

"Come along," she said, clutching Ann's hand. "We are going to take a little walk right now." She knew there was a bus stop somewhere. There was a dirt path that led straight to it. They could take the bus home. Mom could stay here and enjoy chatting with her friends. She'd call her later and tell her to bring Barry home. He was playing in his playpen, with Granny to look after him. He was perfectly safe.

But the girls... What were they getting into their heads? All because of Ewan and his outdoor lifestyle. She didn't want someone else to interfere in her decisions about the children. To question her or challenge her. It was hard enough doing this on her own without the added struggle of alternate views.

"We are going this way."

"But that isn't the way to the center," Stacey protested. "I thought you said we could have apple pie."

"Yes, honey, you can. Later. Now we are going this way." She pulled Ann along, who was reluctant to follow and eyed Stacey with a dubious look.

Stacey said, "Where are you taking us?"

"Come along now, it's a surprise."

Stacey sighed. "I don't like your surprises. Ewan's are much better."

Of course. Because it was always about wild and adventurous things. The irritation burned through her veins like fire. He was a man who had no children of his own. He had ideas that just didn't work for a parent. Because the parent was emotionally invested. Worried about the child. She didn't want her life to become a constant struggle over the children's loyalty. That would be bad for them and for the relationship.

They walked along the dirt path in silence. Ann was looking up at the trees on her side of the path, cocking her head as if she was listening for something.

"What are you doing?" Gina asked eventually.

Ann smiled. "There are woodpeckers here. You can hear them hammering."

Gina hadn't heard anything. Maybe because her anger was consuming all of her attention?

Stacey said, "There are also squirrels. They are very cute. They climb high in the trees, and they are very hard to spot. But Ewan has photos of them on his phone. He knows just where they live."

"He says there is an observation cabin in the woods," Ann said. "That you can see deer from there, early in the morning. Can we go there sometime?"

"I don't think so. I don't want you to be in the forest early in the morning. That is something for grown-ups."

"Ah, Mommy, please?" Ann begged, pulling at her hand.

Stacey said, "Where are we going?"

The path separated into two, one veering more to the left, the other to the right. Gina wasn't sure which one to take to the bus stop. She tried to envision where it was. "Left," she said with more certainty than she felt. "Listen, what is that bird I hear?"

They chatted about birds as they walked, the girls naming all kinds of birds Gina had never heard of before. She couldn't retain them either as her mind was busy running in circles thinking where is that bus stop? It had to lie beside the road she used to reach the center. It was somewhere around here, she was sure. *But once we are there, how long will it take for the bus to come? How will the girls react when they realize we are leaving? Will they make a scene? Will it ruin the entire day?*

To be honest, she was already sorry she had

allowed her irritation to boil over. This impromptu decision to leave was the perfect example of how *not* to solve an issue. She always tried to teach the girls not to walk away from conflict, not to slam the door and hide in their rooms. Now what was she showing them by this behavior? The exact opposite of how she wanted them to behave themselves.

"Mommy?" Stacey pointed ahead. "There is another fork in the path. Where are we going? What route is this? All routes have pointers, you know. Wooden poles with a colored top. Just like a little beanie on top. Once you know what color route you are on, you can use the poles to find your way."

"We are going left," Gina decided. "It's not far anymore. Let's sing a song."

After five songs, they came to another fork in the trail. "I think…" Gina said looking around her. She had a sinking feeling. The trees seemed so tall and imposing. The sun had disappeared behind some clouds and the wind was getting chillier. Or was that just her imagination?

"We have been here before," Ann said. She pointed at a tree with marks on the trunk. "Look, it's just like a face. I saw it earlier."

"You're right," Stacey agreed. "We're going around in circles."

Gina took a deep breath. "I must have made a mistake at the last intersection. Let me check…" She pulled up her phone. No reception. No way to check on a map or…call anyone.

She stared at the screen as panic rose in her chest. She couldn't call her mother to tell her to look after Barry. She couldn't call Granny to ask how she could get back to the center. She couldn't call anyone. She was on her own.

Lost.

In a huge forest that stretched in all directions around her. It was as if she saw herself and the girls from high above, little specks among a vast army of trees. Enemies surrounding them.

Stacey said, "You can't see anything on your phone here, Mommy." She reached into her pocket and produced the compass. "We can see where north is."

"What good is that?" Gina said with dejection flooding her. She was such a bad example to her children. First, she had allowed her anger to take over and bring them into this mess, and now she didn't even know how to get out of it again. She felt like sinking onto a fallen log and hiding her face in her hands.

Stacey held the compass in her palm. Her expression was calm and focused. "North is over there. That means the center is…" She looked around her. "Over there. We have to go in that direction."

Gina gaped at her. "How do you know?"

"Because Ewan taught us to navigate." Stacey shrugged. "He said it was important so we could always find our way back to the center."

"You weren't supposed to go away from the center," Gina said automatically.

"He said we should always stay near it and do what you said. But just in case. In an emergency. Like now."

Gina wanted to say this was not an emergency. But actually it was. Sort of. She had no idea where she was. But if the girls did…

Stacey went ahead proudly carrying the compass. She discussed with Ann at the next intersection. They seemed to get along perfectly. There was no panic. And there were no tears. *She* was the one with the racing heartbeat, not them.

She could tell herself that children didn't see danger. But that was not the case here. These children were equipped to deal with this situation. And Ewan had provided them with that knowledge. He had realized that it was better to understand what you needed to do than just get panicky and run around making mistakes.

He had been right. She had been wrong. Not just about the kids not having to learn survival skills, but also about having to carry the load of raising them alone. She could share it, if she wanted to. If she allowed Ewan to get close to her. It wasn't the differences between them keeping them apart. It was her fear of ending up in trouble again, like she had with the debts. But back then, despite the despair of her situation, she had made it. She had to rely more on her own strength to stay afloat. And at the same time, from that confidence in her own abilities, also allow herself to be helped by others. To admit that life was just better together than alone.

Gina stopped a moment and looked up at the sky. It was mainly blue with a light powdering of clouds. It wasn't threatening at all. And the trees around them weren't an army of enemies but a forest offering shelter to the creatures who lived there. The wonders of nature were all around her, for her to see. If she cared to see them. It was all a matter of perspective.

A hesitant smile broke the tension she felt

in her face. "I think you are really fantastic, girls. Mommy couldn't have navigated with a compass like you can."

"That doesn't matter, Mommy," Ann said with a reassuring smile. "Ewan can teach you too. He is very patient if you don't catch on right away."

Gina's eyes stung. Not with tears of frustration or fear but with a sense of wonder that this could actually be true. That Ewan might also be patient with her. That he might want to…give her a second chance? To do better? To see him for what he was: not a loner, a risk-taking adventurer, but a man with knowledge and skills who was at home in this awesome outdoor world. Who saw the potential dangers and shared about them honestly, equipping people to enjoy nature in peace. He even went out to bring back the lost and wounded. He was wonderful.

Stacey said, "I think I can see an obstacle on the adventure path through the trees. Look, the red thing there."

Ann nodded. "It's part of the hanging bridge." She looked up at Gina. "See, Mommy? We just have to follow the adventure path to get back to the center." Before Gina could respond, she added, "I do hope there will be some apple pie left. I could sure use a big slice."

Gina had to laugh. Relief flooded her and made her want to jump up and whoop. "Me too, darling," she said brushing a hand over her daughter's head. "Me too."

CHAPTER SIXTEEN

EWAN TURNED TO GRANNY, who held Barry in her arms. The little boy was smiling at her and mumbling sounds. If they were meant to be words, Ewan could make out only a few. But he wasn't paying attention either. He was just wondering where Gina was. And the girls. He hadn't seen them in ages. Had they gone along on one of the family tours with a volunteer? To avoid him? He bet the girls would be excited about everything they saw and learned, whoever taught them, but to him it felt like a shame that they weren't spending this special day together.

You have to understand, he corrected himself sternly, *that they aren't your family. You may feel close to them, but if Gina doesn't share that feeling...*

Granny said, "I don't mind looking after this sweet little man at all. Just look at his chubby face. And those hands. He is too cute." She cast him a sly look. "It's almost time for the barbecue. Maybe you can sit with Gina and the girls."

"I bet she wants to eat with her mother. She is here too, you know. I even think I saw Lily and Cade earlier." Ewan had felt uncomfortable facing the brother who had made it clear to him that he expected help in keeping Gina away from harm. No doubt Cade wouldn't think that proclaiming his love for her was fulfilling that order.

"It's wonderful to be together," Granny said. "I am so happy the center brings so much joy to so many people. Oh wait, that is Conan over there. I need to talk to him for a moment. Do you mind?" Without warning, she pushed Barry into Ewan's arms. The little boy pulled a face for a moment, then grinned again, and his hand grabbed for the strap of the binoculars dangling from Ewan's neck. Ewan let him tug at it while he carefully balanced his weight better. "Hey, little guy," he said. "How do you like it here? Have you already seen our giant bear? No, you haven't. Not today anyway." He grinned to himself as he recalled how Barry reacted every time he got near that creature. He widened his eyes and sort of shrank back and then he extended his hands and cried, "Pat, pat, pat."

It was so funny to see. He carried the child through the crowd to reach the bear in the corner. A group of children who were doing the scavenger hunt were just moving on, having answered the question about the bear that was on their flyer. Ewan positioned himself in front of the bear. Barry was still engrossed in examining the leather strap and had paid no attention to where they were moving.

Ewan turned so that Barry could see the bear. "Look there," he said softly.

Barry looked up. His eyes opened wider, and he leaned back in Ewan's arms. He tilted his head as if assessing what this was. Then he extended his chubby arms and called, "Bea. Bea." The *r* was a difficult hurdle for him, and he conveniently left it off.

"Yes, that is a bear. A big bear. They live in the mountains. They walk through the snow like this." Ewan held Barry against his chest as he walked with heavy steps, his feet planted apart. "Where is my honey?" he said in a low growl. "Honey."

"Onee," Barry imitated. "Onee."

"It's too early for honey. So what does the

bear eat? Must he go hungry? What can he find in the forest? What can he eat?"

Barry gave Ewan a questioning look. Then he suddenly looked past him and cried, "Mommy!"

Ewan turned in a jerk. Gina stood close by watching them with an amused smile. Now she stepped up and reached out to place her hand on Barry's back. "Is the bear going to eat Mommy? That is not very nice of the bear."

Barry didn't understand the joke. He just mumbled "Mommy" again and was happy to grab at her necklace.

Ewan felt a little uneasy being caught with her son in his arms and also talking about bears and... It seemed he could do nothing right today. But Gina smiled at him with warmth in her eyes. "The barbecue will start soon," she said. "Do you want to eat with us?"

Ewan felt his jaw drop. He was too shocked for a moment to get any sensible word out. He just nodded. "Sure," he added.

Gina reached out and pulled Barry from his arms. "I don't think he had a nap all day with so many people around. I don't know when he will get grumpy. But it would be a shame to take him home now. Don't you think?"

"Yeah," he said, still not able to understand

what had turned on the light in her eyes. She was suddenly...different. More open, it seemed.

"The girls are outside," she said. "Stacey insisted on teaching other children how to use a compass."

Ewan froze. Gina wasn't supposed to know about that. Well, it wasn't like she couldn't know, but he had meant to prepare her for it. Someday.

But he had delayed too long. She had found out and... Her kindness was probably just the silence before the storm. She'd come over with a smile and started the topic innocently to then explain to him how this was the last thing she had ever wanted. He had to be prepared for it. Not defend himself but apologize.

"Look," he said, "I know I should have discussed it with you first and asked your opinion. And I would have had it been anything other than...these skills. I know how you feel about... Well, you might think it was because I wanted them to do dangerous things. But it is not. It's the other way around. I want them to understand danger and avoid it. Or be prepared to deal with risks when they come across them. Because they will sooner or later and... That is, if they keep coming here. But I hope they will. I mean, I hope you won't tell them they can't come anymore. Because they really like it, and it would be a shame if…"

"Ewan." Gina touched his arm. "It's alright. I saw how Stacey is teaching those kids, and it is amazing to see my wild little girl show this caring side. I…" She swallowed a moment. "I had forgotten she can also be like that. I was only seeing her stunts and thinking she would be hurt someday and… I acted from fear. No, worse even. I *re*acted from fear. I was just caught up in this cycle of trying to avoid every possible risk and…"

"I understand where you're coming from," he assured her.

"Yes, everyone understands that. Mom, Cade, Lily… They all want to protect me. Keep me from harm. They do with me what I do with my children. 'Let me wrap you in tissue paper so you can never be hurt.' It stems from love, but it isn't right. They need to have experiences and learn new things. They have to figure out things for themselves instead of me hovering over them all the time and pulling them away like they are still little. They're growing up and… I have to give them the room to do so. You showed me that." She swallowed again, her features tense. "I must apologize, Ewan, for how I treated you. You are the best thing that ever happened to my family, but I reacted like…you were a problem. You aren't. I am."

"Now I must protest." He put his hand over hers. "You are not a problem. You have never been. To anyone."

Gina bit her lip. "I feel like a burden, often. On Mom, Cade and Lily. They're married and should be together, but there I am with the kids…"

"I am sure they don't feel that way." He squeezed her hand. "Don't talk down about yourself. It is great having you around."

She gave him a hesitant smile. "I'm also glad you helped me believe I could expand my baking business. It's scary but it's worth a try. I love doing it and… It would be a shame if I backed out because I'm just too afraid to even try."

GINA HELD EWAN'S GAZE. She felt like she was saying all the wrong things, but she had to get this out. "I feel like I'm the last person in the world who should be with you. You are strong and bold and adventurous, and you jump into helicopters to go save people's lives and I… have never even been inside a helicopter."

"You can come and look inside sometime.

We can even take a tour. A simple sightseeing tour. Nothing spectacular. Or dangerous. You see, we don't have to be the same. We make a good team just because we are different. We shouldn't try to change each other but embrace the way we are. There is enough common ground. We love the children and want to do what's best for them. We can find a way to do that, together."

She felt the warmth of his hand, saw the tenderness in his eyes. Why was he so kind to her and understanding? He should be angry.

But then again, why had the girls not panicked? Why hadn't they told her that it was her fault that they had gotten lost? Because they had wanted to help her find the way again. They were doing this together. As a team. As a family.

"It doesn't really matter to me what we are going to do, Ewan," she said. "As long as we will be doing it together. I want to spend a whole lot more time with you. Not working as colleagues, but… I mean, also working as colleagues, but foremost I want to explore our friendship and what we feel for each other and…"

She'd never thought she would be in love again. That she would feel what she felt right now. And how right it would seem. That she would actually consider saying these words. But she said them. "I want to date you. I want to get to know everything about you. I want us to become an even better team than we already are. A couple who know each other inside and out, who always have each other's back. Who rely on each other. I want to…just allow myself to be happy again."

As she said it, tears formed in her eyes. That was what it was about. Everybody else had always wanted her to be happy. But she hadn't let herself. She had thought up a thousand reasons why she couldn't be. But underneath it all, she hadn't allowed herself happiness while she had lost so much. As if she was somehow still paying off a debt by feeling bad about everything that had happened. However, right now, she saw she had to let go of that past and reach out for something new. Something different from what she had known but good in its own way. Now, she wanted to accept happiness, embrace it. Be amazed that this was possible. That she was so lucky to have found him.

Ewan smiled down on her. He said softly, "I may not have such a way with words. But I agree with everything you just said. I want to be with you. I want to be there for you. I want you to know that…" He looked at Barry and smiled. "This little boy and the girls can also count on me. You have all found a way into my heart and… I would be proud to be on your team."

"You are already on it." Gina blinked against her tears. "You sneaked into my heart while I didn't even notice. When we were on the adventure trail and you said through the forest phone…"

"Aha." His eyes began to sparkle. "You did hear it correctly. You only pretended you hadn't."

"I wasn't sure. Why would you say that to me? But after that I did look at you differently. I wondered if we could be…"

Ewan leaned down to her. "I think we can." Then he kissed her.

EPILOGUE

"WHERE ARE WE GOING?" Gina asked.

By now she should know Ewan wasn't going to tell her. She had asked last night and this morning when they'd set out, but he hadn't budged. They usually went on trips with the children and Fuzzy, so it was kind of special they were going out alone together today. And into the woods...

She leaned back in the car seat and looked at the trees lining the road, at the way the sunshine filtered through them and turned the moss underneath golden. It was such a beautiful day. The window was open a crack and the clean air flowed in. She had learned to love this place so much. It was like a sanctuary, a haven where she could leave the turmoil of her busy life behind.

Her baking business was really taking off, and she was usually busy with it for three or four days a week. Wednesdays and the weekends were reserved for helping out at the center. Ewan and she sometimes had to compare schedules to look for room to see each other outside of work. But they always made time. On days when she wasn't at the center, they messaged a lot. Or he called her to just say I love you. He might say he wasn't romantic, but he was to her mind.

She looked at her purse in her lap. He had given her a cute little key chain to attach to the strap. It was a small dog that looked just like Fuzzy. He had told her when he had handed it to her that she had actually fallen for the dog first. "I saw it in your eyes when you leaned down to her in Bud's Western store…"

Ah, Bud… He was still in Texas. Like she had expected, he enjoyed his new life so much that he didn't even think about coming back to Heartmont. His store was open again, run by a group of locals who believed it belonged in the town center. Often when Gina passed it and she glanced inside, she remembered how her life had been when she'd worked there, and she was amazed at the changes that had taken place. She felt much more confident, much stronger. Aware of her own abilities. Not just to get things right but also to handle situations when it wasn't going smoothly or something unexpected occurred. Ewan had helped her learn to go with the flow. She always wanted to know everything in advance, but it wasn't possible. In fact, it was quite exhausting. She loved her new, more laid-back attitude.

Oh, at times the old worry could creep back in, and she'd run with it for a while. But then she immediately sensed how her shoulders locked and her neck hurt and the stress just took over. She now knew how to deal with that. Just talk it over with Ewan and he always saw some new perspective. And he could always make her smile.

He turned into a dirt road and parked at the side. "We are continuing on foot from here."

"Okay, perfect." Gina opened the door and got out. She was dressed in green like him so they were camouflaged and could see more wildlife. Slowly, she'd begun to know bird and plant names and to feel more assured recognizing sounds and identifying paw prints in the dirt. In the beginning, Ewan had laughed at her frustration over not getting it right on the first try. "It took me years to learn all this," he had said, patting her arm. "Don't beat yourself up."

She took his hand and they walked down a narrower path. The air was so clean and crisp. Fall was deepening. It was a beautiful time of year. She realized she wasn't worried about the darkness of winter coming. She actually looked forward to having snow fights, building snowmen together, sitting in front of the fire drinking hot chocolate. She looked forward to experiencing every season with Ewan by her side.

The trees thinned, and she could see white shimmering through. It seemed to be the wall of a structure. Not a simple cabin but more like a house. A beautiful white house among the trees. As they drew closer, she could make out more details: the windows with stained glass, the large porch with a beautiful view of the surrounding forest.

"I never knew there was a house here," she said. "It must be amazing to live here. The forest is all around, but still we are only a fifteen-minute drive away from town."

"That's right. This used to be the summer residence of a rich industrialist. He came here from June to September to unwind. They had complete freedom and were still close enough to town to go there for dinner or to see friends. There is a lake just a mile down there for boat trips. His wife did a lot of painting. Part of her work is still exhibited at the museum in Yewcreek."

"I can't really paint, but I can imagine these woods invite you to become creative. They are so majestic."

"Granny knows the people who currently own it. She told me we could have a look around. Also inside." He pulled a key from his pocket.

"Oh, how nice. I can't wait to see it." Gina almost held her breath as they went up the creaking porch steps. There was something special about this house. It was inviting somehow.

Ewan unlocked the door. They stepped into a hallway with antlers on the walls, a carpet in peacock blue and cognac. The stairs had a hand-carved railing with a deer head at the end. Oil paintings of autumnal forests and bubbling brooks adorned the walls.

In the living room area there was a large stone fire place to sit around. Leather couches and club chairs, a large table to have dinner at. The kitchen had wood paneling and lots of blues to lighten it. Gina felt like she had walked into her dream house. "I wish it was possible to stay here for a while, like for a weekend or a holiday," she said. "It has this timeless elegance, this classic feel."

"But also some very nice modern appliances," Ewan pointed out, gesturing around the kitchen. "You could bake here."

"Yes, and have you seen those bookcases?" Gina ambled back into the living room and looked along the bookcases that covered the back wall. They reached up to the ceiling and even had a little movable ladder attached. "There are some gorgeous volumes here, leather-bound."

"Yes, and nature diaries that were kept by older generations," Ewan said, pointing out a whole shelf of green-and-blue-covered books.

"Amazing." Gina sighed. "I'm so grateful we could have a look around."

"Don't you want to look upstairs?"

"At the bedrooms? Wouldn't that be prying?"

"No, they are not living here themselves."

"Okay, I guess."

They went upstairs and looked into the first door on their right. It was a children's bedroom with bunk beds and plenty of room to play. The window gave a wonderful view across the treetops. Gina could hear the birds sing outside.

Then they moved on to the master bedroom with a large double bed and a dresser with a polished brass mirror. The color scheme again included blues. Gina ran her hand over the windowsill. "This is so broad you can sit on it. I love it."

The bathroom had obviously been modernized with a large bathtub and shower area, double sinks and a washing machine and dryer. "There is so much space here," Gina marveled.

There were two more bedrooms that served as guest rooms, Ewan explained. "But, of course," he added, "one of them could also be a room for a toddler."

"A toddler?" Gina asked, still looking around her.

"Yes, a cute little kid like Barry," Ewan said. He came to stand behind her and wrapped his arms around her.

She leaned into him. "Whoever is going to live here is very lucky. It's a wonderful place."

"How would you like to live here?" he whispered in her ear.

For a moment she thought she had misheard, as she had on the forest phone. She heard it, but she didn't dare believe it. It had to be some kind of mistake.

"Me?" she asked.

Ewan laughed softly. "Darling, you don't think I brought you here to have you admire all these delights that are out of reach? Granny says the owners don't want it sitting empty.

She talked to them, and they said they would be willing to rent it to me. To me and my family."

Gina twisted around in his arms. "Really? You mean that?"

"Yes or I wouldn't be saying it."

"But I can't believe it. How did you find such a perfect place where we have the joys of nature all around and are still so close to town? Why would these people want us to live here?"

"Because Granny assured them we will care for the place and would be very happy here. What do you think? The girls can grow up in the middle of nature, but still be close to their grandmother, uncle and aunt. They can go to the ranch often and play there, take care of their animals. Here they will have Fuzzy to look after. You can bake to your heart's delight and deliver to the center and your other customers. I will do my guided tours, the occasional rescue mission, and in my spare time I have to read all those nature dairies. Maybe I can even write a few of my own." He smiled at her. "We can continue the history of the people who lived here. They loved the mountains and the woods and everything that lives there. And so do we."

And so do we. Yes, she could wholeheartedly

agree with that now. Raised on the ranch, she was a country girl at heart who had been swept into a completely different world when she had married Barry and moved to the city. Even there, she had cared for animals and tended a garden, baked often. Here she could do all those things fully immersed in a world that had been his at first, but into which he had welcomed her and shown her around. It was theirs now, to explore and make their own. This house, this amazing house…

She breathed its smell, took in every detail of this moment. The sun flowing in through the window, caressing the wooden floorboards, the chest for toys, the handmade crib in the corner. Barry would be a little too big for it but… Who knew? There might be a little baby one day whom she would lay down to sleep in this very room.

Her heart burst with happiness. Ewan let go of her, and she heard the floorboards creek. As she turned around, he had gone down on bended knee. He had a box in his hand, a small velvet box that was open. A gold ring sat inside, with a sparkling stone in the center. It twinkled at her with a dazzling light.

"Gina…" His eyes overflowed with tenderness. "Do you want to marry me?"

"Yes, oh yes, Ewan, yes!" She jumped into his arms, and he almost lost his balance. They laughed until Gina felt a sting in her eyes. Happy tears, at last. The darkness of the past had subsided, and the skies overhead were blue. He had blown away her sadness and led her back into the light, into a great open space where she could run like a little girl. She no longer had to carry the load alone but could be carefree again, reaching out for his hand and knowing he would be there to grab her when she needed that. In turn, she would be there for him. It wasn't hard. It was the most natural thing to do. It was timeless like the woods around them, like the mountains that watched over their world. That witnessed this precious moment.

"I want to marry you, Ewan McAllister, because I love you so, so much." She brushed her hand over his cheek and leaned in to kiss him.

Ewan whispered, "I love you too," before their lips met, and they didn't have to say anything else. Everything had been said, was understood. They were a team, a family.

From now on, forever.

* * * * *